About the Author

Dr. Keren Obara is a visionary author in the realm of science fiction. With a knack for weaving intricate tales that bridge the gap between the known and the fantastical, Keren takes readers on a mind-bending journey through an uncharted galaxy named the Sigma Galaxy, filled with inter-dimensional possibilities. Keren's captivating narrative style paints vivid landscapes of the future while delving deep into the complexities of human nature and technological evolution. Prepare to be transported to *Cyber Planet XYZ*, a world of fun and adventure.

CYBER PLANET XYZ

Keren Obara

CYBER PLANET XYZ

Vanguard Press

VANGUARD PAPERBACK

© Copyright 2024
Keren Obara

The right of Keren Obara to be identified as author of
this work has been asserted by her in accordance with the
Copyright, Designs and Patents Act 1988.

All Rights Reserved

No reproduction, copy or transmission of this publication
may be made without written permission.
No paragraph of this publication may be reproduced,
copied or transmitted save with the written permission of the publisher, or in
accordance with the provisions
of the Copyright Act 1956 (as amended).

Any person who commits any unauthorised act in relation to this publication
may be liable to criminal prosecution and civil claims for damages.

A CIP catalogue record for this title is available from the British Library.

ISBN 978-1-83794-353-1

This is a work of fiction. Names, characters, businesses, places, events and
incidents are either the products of the author's imagination or used in a
fictitious manner. Any resemblance to actual persons, living or dead, or actual
events is purely coincidental.

Vanguard Press is an imprint of
Pegasus Elliot Mackenzie Publishers Ltd.
www.pegasuspublishers.com

First Published in 2024

Vanguard Press
Sheraton House Castle Park
Cambridge England

Printed & Bound in Great Britain

Acknowledgments

Dedicated to all who encouraged me to shoot for the stars. Dedicated to all who wish to shoot for the stars. And most of all, dedicated to you, the reader, who has such a beautiful spark in your heart that you attracted this book to you.

CYBΣR PLANΣT XYZ:
Sigma Space Racers

The Sigma Space Race: An event where the best space car racers from different galaxies compete in a tournament that lasts the span of four Earthian months, April to July. The sigma space race takes place in the Sigma Galaxy, on Cyber Planet XYZ—the most advanced planet in the Cosmos.

The sigma space race is made up of three quarters:

The interplanetary quarter – where the best racers of each galaxy race against each other to enter in the intergalactic quarter. Six teams from each galaxy qualify from this round.

The intergalactic quarter – where the galactic teams that qualified from the first quarter go against racers from other galaxies. Six teams will qualify from this round and move on to the final quarter.

The final quarter – the six teams that qualified in the intergalactic quarter battle each other in the semifinals and the finals to find out who the real sigma space race champions are.

Δ **Addition**: Points are earned based on the finishing position of one's team. The teams with the lowest points are eliminated. The teams with the highest points qualify.

Δ **In the final quarter**, the sigma space racing champions are announced.

Δ Becoming a sigma space race champion automatically makes one a diplomat of the Cosmos.

Δ **As a diplomat**, the sigma space race champions sign a contract to represent the Cosmos in inter-universal relations. Failure to do so is punishable by law.

Prologue

One moment, Ken-Yah was racing through swinging pendulum axes; the other moment, she was spiraling downward toward the heat of the Icarus star.

Ken-Yah, ever the clever thinker, pressed a button on her watch that created a portal under the car.

The car flew into a cosmopolitan high-tech planet.

Ken-Yah screamed as the car spiraled through the skyline of a highly advanced planet.

All around the car, robots flew around Cyber City. She tried her best to maneuver over the busy skyline and not hit any of the robots that flew past them.

She was flying through the skyline of the one and only Cyber Planet XYZ. The most famous planet in the Cosmos.

How did she reach that point? Well, it all started because of the curiosity of one girl, Sha-Nah.

Chapter One

Location: Intergalactic Kaizen School Earth 2

Sha-Nah adjusted her Kaizen tracksuit.

Kaizens[1] were known as the most gifted teens on Earth, as they had the ability to enhance their physical abilities using a brain chip.

She tied her big, fluffy hair in two long French braids and wore her signature cap.

Sha-Nah practiced a set of martial arts moves as she looked in the mirror. She, then, walked to a robotic measuring scale at the corner of the room.

"1.5% body fat," the robot spoke.

"Good job, Sha-Nah," she muttered to herself. She swung a flying kick into the air one more time and released a series of punches in the air.

The speaker in her room made a clicking noise that meant a message from the principal was coming in.

"Good morning, Class 1B Kaizens, this is Principal Eunheyyh speaking. As you know, for the first week of school, you have mainly activities, not classes. The

---

[1] Kaizen—a Kaizen student from the Central Corporate Province Earth 2

students of Class 1A—you might know some of them; Zenia, Olly, Kazan, Lilith—begin Kaizen training immediately.

"However, for Class 1B, you will have joint activities with the Earthian Milky Way School. We'll be traveling away from the Central Corporate Province to the Earth Main Province. The Kaizen students will stay in a dorm reserved just for them, on the school campus of the Earthian Milky Way School. The private jet will leave at exactly eight a.m. sharp."

"Another boring school trip," Sha-Nah said. "When is something interesting going to happen?"

It seemed as though fate heard Sha-Nah's request for something interesting to happen. Suddenly, one of the screens in the corner of her room lit pink with a notification.

A voice spoke, "Your subscription to the Annual Sigma Space Race broadcast has been authorized. You will be granted access to watch the full season of events. Today, teams from the Milky Way Galaxy will compete in round one try-outs for a chance to enter the prestigious sigma space race. Don't miss it!"

"Yes!" Sha-Nah turned on her phone to send a voice note to her group chat of friends. "Six p.m., this evening." As soon as she sent the voice note, there was a plethora of replies as her friends joked around.

She chuckled as she read them. "Idiots." She laughed to herself as she looked in the mirror and flexed her arm muscle one last time before winking at herself, her brown eyes twinkling with excitement.

Sha-Nah made her way outside. Her tracksuit looked really cool.

Her friends were already in the jet. She walked in.

The jet flew to the Earthian Milky Way School.

Sha-Nah and her friends made their way into the school and were handed flyers.

Unlike the orderly Intergalactic Kaizen School, the Earthian Milky Way School was less orderly, with a more casual and freestyle vibe to it. The students looked like they had a lot of freedom there.

A lecturer spoke to Sha-Nah and her friends. "These flyers will show you the inter-school programs for the next week and where your dorms are." The Kaizens thanked her politely and took the flyers.

The students of the Earthian Milky Way School all came out of their classes to see the Kaizens.

A student whispered to another as she stood by her locker. "I can't believe we actually get to interact with Kaizens."

"They're all ripped; they must train a lot..."

"Do you think they could tell us about the brain chip?"

"I'd sure like to know..."

The bell rang. It was time for Sha-Nah to head to her program of the day.

Sha-Nah jogged across the hallway of the school building almost absent-mindedly. She accidentally collided into another student. Papers and books scattered all over the floor.

The student she bumped into was a really pretty girl with thick hair, chocolate skin, and purple eyes.

"Oh, my goodness." Sha-Nah helped the purple-eyed girl pick her books up. "I'm so sorry. Are you okay?"

The purple-eyed girl nodded; she breathed heavily, as though she had been doing something extremely energetic.

"Are you okay?" Sha-Nah asked.

"I have to go," the purple-eyed girl said. She got up quickly and ran outside the school building.

After she ran away, Sha-Nah looked down at the floor; the girl had forgotten one of her papers.

Sha-Nah picked it up and brought it closer to her face. Her brows furrowed as she looked in curiosity. It was a ticket.

The ticket was to the Sigma Space Race tryouts set to take place that day.

Sha-Nah looked at the direction in which the purple-eyed girl ran with a curious expression on her face.

*

After the first interschool program, Sha-Nah and her friend Bjørn spoke in the hallway. They stood by the window, facing the large field outside.

Bjørn had curly red hair and freckles. Sha-Nah always appreciated his charm and smile. All the girls always cooed at his cuteness.

He and Sha-Nah looked at a magazine. Bjørn's charm is what made him the poster boy for the brand *The Female Gaze* an intergalactic magazine for teenagers—mostly concentrated on sports, fashion, and other popular subjects in the Cosmos.

The Female Gaze headquarters was in the Andromeda Galaxy, and it was owned by popular fashion designer—Astrid Venus, who designed the Kaizen outfits each year as well as the Sigma Space Racer outfits. Her designs made her the richest woman in the Cosmos. With only one close competitor for the spot—Ramona Ratna, mother of Kazan Ratna.[2]

As Sha-Nah and Bjørn talked, Sha-Nah saw the girl she bumped into earlier. The purple-eyed girl from earlier walked by Sha-Nah and Bjørn. She wore a racing suit with the words 'Earth School Racing Club' written on it.

The purple-eyed girl walked into the hallway, looked around her, and then eventually walked down a flight of stairs. Sha-Nah's curiosity was drawn toward the purple-eyed girl.

Suddenly, both Sha-Nah and Bjørn's watches buzzed. They looked at their wrists. Their watches showed a mini hologram of the phrase 'time for soccer match'.

Sha-Nah and Bjørn looked excitedly at each other before they ran down the hallway to change into their soccer outfits.

---

[2] Kazan Ratna—popular student at the Intergalactic Kaizen School.

They met up with their Kaizen friends as they walked to the soccer field.

At lunch, they all sat at a table and chatted excitedly about the soccer match that they had just had.

As they joked around, Sha-Nah spotted the purple-eyed girl once again.

She sat staring at a cupcake.

Is that all she's having for lunch?

Sha-Nah looked at her for a while longer before finally deciding to approach her and apologize for bumping into her.

She walked over to where the girl sat and cleared her voice before she spoke.

"Hello there. I'd like to apologize once again for bumping into you earlier. I hope you're all right," she spoke.

"Oh cool, no worries," the girl replied with a slight smile.

"I'm Sha-Nah," she introduced. "What's your name?"

"I'm Ken-Yah," the purple-eyed girl replied.

"Nice to meet you, Ken-Yah," Sha-Nah said.

"Thank you, have a nice day," Ken-Yah replied.

As Sha-Nah walked away, it took Ken-Yah a moment to get back to what she was trying to do. Eat.

She sighed for a moment before getting up and leaving the cupcake behind.

Ken-Yah turned on a mini-virtual screen from on watch. A series of numbers appeared on the screen.

"Perfect," she said.

You see, Ken-Yah had a secret that no one knew. She had created a portal machine that let her travel anywhere she wanted.

That's how she secretly snuck out of school.

Ken-Yah locked herself in a room and typed a code into the virtual screen.

A portal opened, and she entered it.

She landed in a desert.

Sahara Desert—Earth 1:

A fleet of Sand Racing Cars drove past her. The engines roared as the glorious sun of the Sahara Desert shined down on the Berber Sand Racers and Tuareg nomads who were racing side by side. They cruised through the desert sand and the hot scorching sun of the Sahara gave them lots of energy. They went at maximum speed, some of them bending the cars to drive on only two tires. The fleet of Berber Sand Racers consisted of almost a hundred cars designed for the desert. They wore Indigo Turbans, the traditional Berber/Tuareg attire.

They cheered and shouted as they raced forward. One Amazigh Racer held her hand out to Ken-Yah. She took it and jumped into the car. She took the driving seat and screamed as she pressed the accelerator. The car went at a drastic speed and took the first position in the fleet of Sand Racers.

After the race, Ken-Yah got out of the car and ran through the desert excitedly. She said goodbye to her Sand

Racer friend and made her way to a dome structure labeled, "Intergalactic skater's Association."

She put up her I.D. to the entrance and was immediately let in. There was a large skateboarding rink in the dome, the best one on Earth 1. It was also a hotel, where the best skate boarders in the galaxy stayed during tournaments and competitions.

She scanned the area looking for someone. There he was. Her skater boyfriend, Vaughn. She immediately spotted him with a couple of friends. They were spending the day on Earth 1, but they were all from Vaporwave City on Earth 2.

As soon as Vaughn saw Ken-Yah, he walked to her.

Every time she saw him, she felt extremely thirsty, and not for water. Vaughn was the peak definition of hot and sexy. At six feet tall, he had an amazing body because he always worked out. His curly hair was blondish and rested silkily on his forehead. Just brushing by his blue droopy "kiss-me eyes" and sculpted jawline. To Ken-Yah, his eyes said more than just "kiss me," and every time she saw him, her mind flooded with naughty things. She looked up at him; he looked sexy, running his hands through his curly blondish hair. His cheeks were pink and flustered, which always happened when he saw her.

"Ken-Yah..." he said.

"Vaughn..." she replied.

He placed his hand on her cheek and bent down to kiss her. They had not seen each other in a week, and that felt like hell for them because they both had strong urges they had to fulfill. Ken-Yah felt her senses tingling. She snuck her tongue in between his lips and licked the roof of his mouth before taking his whole bottom lip and nibbling on it. Vaughn let out a slight 'uh' because he had missed that so much. She reached her hand into the pocket of his sweatpants and brushed along the 'tip' of his you know what.

Vaughn lost his breath and accidentally dropped his skateboard.

"Dude! Get a room!" Vaughn's friend—Dionysus—yelled all the way from the skating rink.

Vaughn and Ken-Yah didn't pay him any attention. But they did exactly that, they hung out in Vaughn's hotel room that whole evening. The beautiful sunset peered into their room. Vaughn kept on kissing Ken-Yah's cheek as she looked at holograms of space racing cars.

All advanced space racing car formulas were named the 333 model and 444 model. She wished deep in her heart that she could own one of those. Ken-Yah loved space racing so much; it was her passion, her calling in life. She could feel it.

Vaughn loved seeing her excited about what she loved. It made him feel happy. He was in his senior year of high school, and his parents planned for him to move away after graduating. That meant that he'd have to leave Ken-Yah, who was two years below him. He remembered a conversation he had had with her.

"They want me to move away, but I don't want to leave you," Vaughn said to Ken-Yah one night, as they watched the stars together on the rooftop of her house.

Ken-Yah sat up and looked at him. Her purple eyes shined in a way that made his heart melt.

"I don't want you to hold yourself back because of me," Ken-Yah said to him.

A comet shower began above them. The whole night sky was filled with lights.

Vaughn looked into Ken-Yah's eyes and felt something he had never felt before.

That was the night he knew he had fallen in love with her.

"Shit…" he said to himself.

"Wow," Ken-Yah said as she looked at more space racing cars. Vaughn snapped back to the present moment.

Her purple eyes glowed with awe as she looked at one particular 333 model.

"You like it?" Vaughn asked.

"I love it," Ken-Yah replied.

"I'll get it for you," Vaughn said. "Would you like that?"

"Yeah, I would," Ken-Yah replied absent-mindedly as she continued to marvel at the purple space racing cars.

Vaughn logged on to his computer and began to stream a game online, for his audience of billions across the Cosmos. Yeah, Vaughn was pretty famous and well known. He started his career gaming but blew up because of his good looks. He caught the attention of

"Showstopper," one of the biggest fashion labels in the Cosmos, owned by Ramona Ratna. That is how he became one of the youngest billionaires from Earth 2.

He was versing his friends Dionysus and Kazan Ratna in the online game. However, he was distracted by Ken-Yah sitting in his lap, so Dionysus killed off his character.

"Fuck you, Dionysus," Vaughn said.

Dionysus could be seen laughing on the other side of the stream.

The game ended and Vaughn turned his attention back to Ken-Yah. He was about to kiss her when there was a knock at the door.

"That must be Jarvien and Santino," Vaughn said as he walked to open the door.

He opened the door and there they were, Jarvien and Santino—Vaughn's friends from Vaporwave City—looking stylish as they always did.

Jarvien was a famous fashion influencer and Santino was a tech startup CEO in Vaporwave City. They had just graduated senior year of high school and were flying high. The same high school that Vaughn was about to graduate from. Vaughn had invited them to hang out since they were in the hotel for the night.

They looked extremely stylish; Jarvien always managed to look good, and he definitely had an influence on Santino's style.

Santino fist bumped Vaughn as he entered. The two were gym buddies and always got gains together. They were both six feet two, so they towered over Ken-Yah and Jarvien.

"How are you guys?" Jarvien asked as Ken-Yah hugged him excitedly. The two were super close, like brother and sister.

"We're chilling," Vaughn replied.

"I'm looking at super cool cars," Ken-Yah replied as she expanded the hologram of the 333 model that had caught her attention.

Jarvien smiled at her cuteness.

"Oh, we got one of those," Santino said.

"For real?" Ken-Yah and Vaughn asked at the same time.

"Yeah, wanna go for a ride?" Jarvien asked as he took out a set of purple keys from his pocket.

Ken-Yah excitedly grabbed the keys and ran out.

They went for a ride through the dessert with the glittering night sky above them.

Ken-Yah laughed in excitement as the car cruised through the sand. Vaughn smiled and laughed as well.

Santino and Jarvien were in the back seats. Jarvien was having a full-on panic attack while Santino was unfazed. He had gotten used to the antics of the two teenagers.

"I got a crazy idea," Ken-Yah said. "Let's go watch the Sigma Space Race tryouts on Kepler 452b."

Santino checked his watch.

"I'm down for that," Vaughn said. They looked at Jarvien and Santino.

"Ah, what the heck!" Jarvien threw his hands in the air. "Let's do it."

*

Next thing, the two couples were in the Coliseum of Kepler 452b, cheering the space racers on. They all had 444 model type space racing vessels, and Ken-Yah absolutely loved every bit of it. The race was just about to start.

"Welcome to the Milky Way Try Outs for the Annual Sigma Space Race!" the hologram of a classy-looking man spoke as he hovered over a coliseum filled with a large crowd that cheered and roared with excitement as fireworks blasted above them.

There was a high-tech racetrack, with four space vessels rumbling at the engines. The pilots each had determined faces as they clutched their controls tight.

"Today, we have three teams from the Milky Way Galaxy fighting for a chance to participate in the race. In total, the contestants trying out from the Milky Way Galaxy amount to nine teams. There will be three races each to determine which three teams will get to compete in the Sigma Space Race." The crowd cheered.

"In the first lane, from planet Kepler 422b of the Milky Way Galaxy, we have the crowd's favorite, Team Su-Ha and Jake." The crowd cheered, loudly and enthusiastically.

Su-Ha clutched the controls. "It's game time," she mouthed to herself. "No body's going to take the prize away from me this time. Victory will be mine, and I'll do anything to make sure of that." She looked up at the hologram of a trophy above her. "That prize shall be mine."

"In lane two, we have Team Gemini and Artemis, from Planet Venus of the Milky Way." The crowd cheered. Gemini and Artemis looked over at Su-Ha and Jake. Su-Ha gave them the death stare.

"In lane three, we have Rhocancrians E-1 and E-2." The crowd fell silent.

The Rhocancrians were pure balls of viscous matter, and they tended to sometimes make things a bit awkward by spilling gooey matter all over the racetrack.

"And now, let the countdown begin." The crowd counted with the host. "Ready!"

The engines rumbled, the racers focusing heavily on the lane.

"Set!"

Su-ha stared at the racetrack, determined. Jake was relaxed as always, a juxtaposition between the two. Gemini and Artemis fixed their special controls that gave them competitive edge. The Rhocancrians, well, the Rhocancrians simply remained still.

"Go!"

The racers took off with blasting speed. They drifted ahead on the racetrack, constantly passing each other. Everyone watched intently. Su-ha changed gears and controls as she accelerated forward. Gemini and Artemis were just as fast as Su-Ha and Jake. The Rhocancrians raced at a fast pace as well.

Meanwhile, Sha-Nah watched the race from the common room in the Earthian Milky Way School with her Kaizen friends. "Gemini and Artemis' competitive strategy lies in the amount of work they put into their battleship racers. They're the best mechanics in the Milky Way with advanced knowledge on how to effectively implement Venus' natural resources into extremely volatile and efficient systems," she spoke.

Gemini and Artemis bypassed Su-Ha and Jake, taking the number one spot, leaving both Su-Ha and Jake and the Rhocancrians far behind by miles. The crowd cheered.

"They're going to win," someone in the common room said.

"No," Sha-Nah said. "They're going to lose."

*

On the racetrack, the battleship racers blasted on, with Su-Ha and Jake last, the Rhocancrians second, Gemini and Artemis in first place.

Su-ha began to laugh excitedly.

"Here we go," Jake said calmly and nonchalantly as he worked on a few codes within the battleship racer.

Su-Ha laughed louder as she picked up a flare gun and climbed out of the window onto the top of the battleship.

She shot her flare gun up into the sky; a line of pink smoke blasted into several pink glittery pixels as she laughed in delight. The race was almost coming to an end; only ten seconds were left. Su-Ha and Jake had trailed way too far behind to the point that it was simply pitiful.

Su-Ha jumped back into the seat.

Jake finalized his coding process into the controls and process functioning of their battleship racer. "Loaded hundred percent. Here we go."

Su-ha held the staring wheel as their battleship racer blasted forward at light speed and bypassed their two opponents in a second, finishing in first place.

The crowd cheered loudly as the winning team label was given to Su-Ha and Jake.

Su-ha smiled brightly and cheered as the crowd cheered for her and her boyfriend.

The Rhocancrians finished second, Gemini and Artemis last.

"Ladies and gentlemen, the winners of this race—Team Su-Ha and Jake!" The crowd cheered more.

Su-Ha and Jake climbed up to receive the trophy.

"Su-Ha and Jake! Su-Ha and Jake!" the crowd chanted. Su-ha waved to all of them and turned around with her hands in the air, chanting with them.

As soon as the match was done, the Kaizen students looked at each other.

Half of them had placed their bets on Gemini and Artemis, half of them had placed their bets on Su-Ha and

Jake. Sha-Nah had a smirk on her face as she had betted on the right team.

Meanwhile, on Kepler 452b, Ken-Yah, Vaughn, Jarvien, and Santino were leaving the coliseum.

They left through the V.I.P. route. The space racers left through the same route. Cameras were flashing; paparazzi were lined up, trying to get the best pictures of the space racers.

As soon as they saw Vaughn, Jarvien, and Santino, they went crazy. Vaughn held Ken-Yah's hand firmly as they walked through the flashing lights.

After leaving Kepler 452b, Ken-Yah said goodbye to Vaughn. He watched her walk into a portal before he himself made his way back to Vaporwave City.

Ken-Yah returned back to the Earthian Milky Way School and ran to her dorm room. There was always a roll call at night so she couldn't spend the night with Vaughn or else the school would know that she was sneaking out.

When Jarvien and Santino got back to their hotel room, Jarvien was tired. He yawned. Santino kissed him. Jarvien always felt small and safe in Santino's arms.

"You okay?" Santino asked Jarvien.

"I'm okay," Jarvien replied.

"I love you," Santino said.

"I love you too," Jarvien said, feeling himself absolutely loved and adored by his soulmate. He always knew he would be all right and well taken care of. After all, Santino was naturally a caregiver.

Santino helped Jarvien take off his shoes as Jarvien scrolled through his phone. Jarvien saw something that caught his attention.

"Santino," Jarvien said.

"Hmm?" Santino asked.

Jarvien showed him the phone screen.

"Chase…" Jarvien said to Santino.

It was a missing person's announcement of someone they knew who had gone missing in high school. His name was Chase. But everyone knew him by his gamer name—Fulcrum, which he used while streaming online. He was friends with them in high school. But one day, he suddenly disappeared with no trace.

"It's been two years," Santino said.

"I know," Jarvien replied. "I just have a bad feeling about it, still."

"I understand you," Santino replied. "Just put the phone away and focus on me." He lifted Jarvien's chin and looked into his eyes.

"Remember what we talked about," Santino said to him. "Don't stress about anything that is beyond your control. Your mental health is important to me." He kissed Jarvien's forehead.

"And every time you don't control your anxiety, your powers go out of control, remember?" Santino said.

Jarvien turned his phone off and smiled at Santino. Santino smiled back; it was a loving and endearing smile.

*

Sha-Nah sat by herself as she analyzed the race that had just happened on Kepler 452b. "What I've observed watching Su-Ha and Jake is that while opponents normally formulate winning strategies beforehand, they are somehow able to formulate a plan right on spot, within seconds. One needs to have quick and sharp processing skills to pull such a risk off."

She sat in the common room as she replayed the recorded video of the race over and over. She kept on rewinding back to the part just right before Su-Ha and Jake took the winning spot.

Eventually, she settled into her own silence. She sighed. She felt bored.

"Insomnia… once again."

She got up and walked to the fridge. She picked out a cupcake and pulled out a candle from her pocket. She walked to the window and placed the cupcake on the frame.

She placed the candle in the cupcake. Waving her hand over the candle, a flame ignited.

"Happy birthday, Sha-Nah," she said to herself. "Make a wish, Sha-Nah."

She looked at the stars.

"I wish for something exciting to happen in my life." She blew out the candles.

Chapter Two

The next day Sha-Nah walked down the hallway in her soccer outfit; she watched a virtual screen in front of her that simulated a soccer match. She had planned to play soccer with her friends, read a bit, and then practice martial arts.

Bjørn and her other friends joined her; they walked together, joking and laughing. She stopped at her locker to collect something, her friends chattering behind her. She laughed at what they were saying.

Suddenly, someone caught Bjørn's eye, and he stared across the hallway. Sha-Nah looked behind to see what Bjørn was looking at.

There she was, the purple-eyed girl, dressed in racing attire as she walked past them, with a helmet in her hands. Sha-Nah and her friends looked at Ken-Yah.

She walked down the stairs.

Ken-Yah walked to the school racetrack. It was an important day for the racing team.

"Listen up," the racing coach spoke.

"For those who performed horribly in the previous test, I will not tolerate any of your mediocrity anymore." He looked directly at Ken-Yah. She tried her best to keep a straight face on, although the comment and insinuation hurt her. "The only reason one would fail at this class is due to extreme laziness."

The school space racing team stood in a row, consisting of seven girls.

Their racecars were parked behind them.

On that day, Earthian officials visited the school to scout for talented young racers that could possibly bring prestige to Earth on the intergalactic racing scene.

"I told you about this at the start of the school year," the racing coach spoke.

"Joining us today are scouts from Earth Space Racing Institute. They are here to spot potential racers to represent Earth in future Sigma Space races."

He paused and walked around, eyeing the students.

"They are putting together an official team of racers that they can manage efficiently. Instead of just solo teams trying out for the Sigma Space Races, they plan to recruit and manage the best racers on this planet to have a more organized and centralized strategy toward an Earthian team winning the grand prize of the Sigma Space Race. This will bring political power to Earth and improve our intergalactic relations with the Sigma Galaxy." He paused. "Some of you only know how to fail." He looked straight at Ken-Yah. "You better not embarrass me today."

The coach continued to speak. "The officials are here to observe this team. They will be taking note of your skills. If you showcase your best skills, you stand a chance to get scouted and trained to represent Earth."

The other students clapped excitedly. Ken-Yah stood still. She gulped; an uneasy feeling took over her. She felt nervous and nauseous.

"We will put into practice the techniques you have learnt, starting with the trail braking technique. Understood?" the coach spoke.

"Yes, sir," they replied.

"I hope you all revised the techniques and took extra time during the weekend to read about the physics and engineering behind them," he spoke.

"Yes, sir," they all replied.

Ken-Yah's eyes widened. She had been too busy over the weekend with her shenanigans.

"We'll start with the trail braking technique," he spoke. "Now, who can tell me what trail braking is?"

"Sir." One of the girls raised her hand. She was given permission to speak. "Trail braking is the technique of lightened, yet continuous braking while turning into a corner of the racetrack."

Another student raised her hand. "Sir, one interesting concept I came across during my practice is the fact that this technique enables the racer to manipulate the car's mass in order to aid corner entry."

"Exactly," he replied. "If you'll ever race in the big leagues, you'll realize those corners are nothing to play with, okay? This is a difficult technique to get consistently right. A lot of effort will be required to ensure you get the most out of your engines and tires at corner entry."

The scouts from the Earth Space Racing Institute watched intently.

The students put on their helmets as they got into their racing cars and started their engines. Ready. Set. Go. The cars took off at full speed. The other girls sped off fast, leaving Ken-Yah in the last place.

Ken-Yah realized that someone had tampered with her racing car. There was something wrong with it.

"Someone messed with my car," she said to herself.

The student in first place successfully trail-braked and sped off to the finish line. The other students did so as well.

It was Ken-Yah's turn to trail brake.

However, when she reached the corner of the racetrack, she faltered. The car's wheels turned out of control, and she spun off the racetrack.

Thankfully, for her, the school's safety AI system was designed to create a bubble-like void around any vehicle that spun out of control on the racetrack.

Her vehicle stopped mid-air and gently glided back down.

She stepped out of the car to disappointed and disapproving looks from her coach and the Earthian officials.

The girls in her team were laughing at her. She, then, realized that they had messed with her car.

"Ken-Yah, did you do any practice or reading before this class?" the coach asked.

"Yes, I did," Ken-Yah said.

"Do you think I'm stupid?" The coach shouted at her. "You good-for-nothing pathetic little girl. You're lazy, and you'll never amount to anything."

"That's it, you're out. Don't come back to this class again," he yelled and dismissed her away.

She was too stunned to speak, frozen in place, unable to ask for a second chance, which she had done countless times before.

The coach turned back to her. "Get out of here!" he spat. "You're making me look bad in front of the scouts from the Earth Space Racing Institute. Just get lost. You're a slacker. You'll never be a serious racer. You'll never amount to anything. You're not wanted here. You'll never be wanted anywhere. Get out of my sight."

Ken-Yah walked away.

Sha-Nah watched from the window with her friends.

*

Ken-Yah sat in one of the stalls of the bathroom.

Suddenly, she heard a group of people entering the bathroom. It was the girls from the racing team.

"I can't believe we were all approached by the Earth Space Racing Scouts! Good job, girls, let's keep working hard." She heard one of them speaking.

"If I ever get the chance to compete in the Sigma Space Race, that'll be the time of my life," one of them said.

"Me too," they all squealed excitedly.

"I think, we're all going to be Sigma Space Race Champions," one girl said.

"What about the Ken-Yah girl? Do you think she's okay?" one of them asked.

"Who cares about her?" one girl replied. "She's weird; she's always somewhere doing something sus. I think she sneaks out of school sometimes. And what's up with that robot arm? What a freak."

"Yeah, nobody even likes her."

"I'm surprised she stuck it out this long. She's the laziest racer and worst student on this team. She's always missing practice."

"Yeah, she's the worst racer I've seen too. The coach doesn't even like her," another added.

"She's always failing at the theory part of this class too. She's a bit slow if you ask me."

"There's no way she'll ever be a Sigma Space Racer."

"She's already embarrassed herself countless times."

"Yeah, like in middle school, when she had a crush on that one guy, and he wanted nothing to do with her."

"And on Valentine's Day, it was her that bought him flowers and chocolates." One girl laughed.

"Oh, yeah... and he rejected the flowers and chocolates."

"That girl is a reject, nothing good will ever happen to her." The girls laughed and walked out of the bathroom.

Ken-Yah sat in silence. "All this time, I've been nothing but nice to them. What did I ever do to them?" she asked herself.

After a few minutes, she got up out of the stall and made her way to the sink.

Looking at herself in the mirror, she wiped the tears from her purple eyes and washed her face.

She walked out of the bathroom and headed out toward the stairs.

Just as she turned, she nearly bumped into someone. She jumped in fight and was visibly shaken. She stumbled back and fell.

"Are you okay?" Sha-Nah asked, looking sincerely concerned.

Sha-Nah stood in front of her in her soccer outfit, with a concerned expression on her face.

"I'm okay," Ken-Yah said before walking away.

Sha-Nah looked at her in curiosity as she ran off. She shrugged and stepped forward. She noticed a piece of paper that Ken-Yah had dropped once again. The paper had a quote written on it. It was an augmented ticket.

'Third Sigma Space Try-outs on Kepler 452 b. Six p.m. Earthian time.

Ticket number 999.'

Sha-Nah held the ticket, her brows furrowed as she walked ahead into the hallway.

A hunch told her to look outside the window, and so she did.

She saw Ken-Yah walking to the school shed that was not in use.

That evening in Sha-Nah's dorm, a hologram floated in the middle of the room, displaying a racetrack.

Sha-Nah and her friends each wrote down their bets for the expected winner into a computer system that would later list the names of those who betted on the winning team.

They watched the race eagerly, each of them cheering for their teams as they watched the events unfold.

They all watched the race eagerly as they placed their bets on the teams they expected to win.

Sha-nah smirked; she had bet on the right team.

She high-fived Bjørn, who had betted on the same team as well.

The all sat around for a game of cards afterward. They had fun as they laughed and joked around.

Later that night, when everyone had gone back to sleep, Sha-Nah rewatched the race on a large screen as she always did.

She kept on rewinding, and each time she did, she slowed the video down to watch the moment at a slower pace.

She repeatedly did so until she noticed something interesting away from the race, in the seats.

She slowed down even more and walked closer to the screen so that she could tell if she was seeing right.

On the screen, in the audience, there was someone who looked familiar.

Sha-Nah rubbed her eyes to make sure she was seeing correctly.

"Ken-Yah…" she said to herself as she moved even closer to the screen and zoomed in more. It was Ken-Yah.

"No way," she said, looking at the screen. She squinted her eyes and looked again. "It's her."

She looked away, baffled, and then looked again. Her eyes scanned the screen. Sha-Nah began to think out loud.

"She must have travelled to Kepler 452b during school hours. She must have an interplanetary portal device of some sort that enables her to travel that quickly.

"If she's travelling that freely, she must be breaking some interplanetary travel laws. A student under eighteen needs to be licensed and regulated to use an interplanetary portal device. But then again, it's Earth, there're loopholes to everything."

Chapter Three

The next day at school, Sha-Nah casually hung out with her friends. She smiled and joked around until she saw Ken-Yah again, walking to a locker. Her thick hair, purple eyes, and stoic expression made her appearance even more alluring. She was in a racing suit. She had a determined look in her purple eyes and moved as though it was only her in the hallway.

Ken-Yah got her bag from her locker and made her way toward a door that led to a downward flight of stairs.

She slid down the handles of the stairs quietly to make no noise. Sha-Nah walked to a window and looked out into the field.

She saw Ken-Yah walking to the shed once again.

That night, Sha-Nah lay on her bed as she played a racing video game. She won the race with a new high score. She then placed the video game on the bed and headed toward the window to look outside.

The sky was starry. She looked at the shed down below and remembered that she had seen Ken-Yah enter it on multiple occasions.

Curiosity took over Sha-Nah. She decided to leave her room and walk out of the dorm.

Once she was outside, she ran to the shed. Anticipation ran through her as she reached closer and closer and, eventually, grabbed the handle of the door.

Immediately, she entered, her eyes widened.

In front of a space racing car, floated a medium sized blue hole. Her mouth hung open as she walked closer to it, surprised beyond belief.

It's not an interplanetary portal device as I thought, but she's got an entire wormhole in here…

Before she could wrap her head around what she was seeing, she heard footsteps approaching the shed. She looked around for where to hide, but nothing was suitable.

She quickly opened the trunk of the space-racing car and closed herself inside it.

Ken-Yah entered the shed.

She looked around and squinted her eyes suspiciously. Looking around the shed, she made sure that nothing was out of the ordinary. She then observed her space-racing car. She lightly touched the rims and then stared ahead at the portal in front of her.

"Perfect," she said to herself. She smiled lightly as she turned on a device.

A series of numbers appeared on a screen in front of her. She began to code certain commands on the screen. Her coding speed quickened as her eyes scanned the numbers intricately.

After her coding process was done, the screen disappeared, and she entered the space-racing car. The wormhole began to spin.

She braced herself. The car blasted through the portal at an intense speed. The portal then closed as Ken-Yah travelled at light speed. She looked ahead in delight as neon lights passed her by. Sha-Nah in the trunk didn't know what was going on.

Ken-Yah laughed cheerfully.

Ahead of the space-racing car, an opening appeared. Ken-Yah looked on enthusiastically, as she flew out of the portal into an atmosphere filled with space shuttles, vessels, and buildings that orbited around a single star.

"Welcome to the Icarus solar system, the trading and finance hub of the Cygnus Galaxy," a hologram of a woman spoke right in front of Ken-Yah's space racing car. "Please, enjoy your stay."

All around her hovered various neon advertisements and holograms directing visitors to banks, casinos, and finance institutes situated in dynamic buildings and state of the art space travel vessels.

Ken-Yah spotted a large fancy building in the distance, just above the Icarus star. She flew directly to it. It was a fancy hotel—Hotel Icarus.

She parked her space-racing car in the parking lot and got out to make her way to the entrance of the large complex. Before she could enter, she was stopped by two large men.

"Identification please," one of the men spoke.

Ken-Yah pressed a button on her watch; a picture of her appeared alongside an identification profile.

| **Name**: Ken-Yah |
| **Origin**: Earthian (Category: Melanated) |
| **Occupation**: Racer for hire |
| **Visitor Status**: Accepted |

The door opened and she was able to enter. The atmosphere in the lobby was fancy, with different guests going about their business. Ken-Yah walked to the reception.

"Greetings, dear guest," a robot spoke. "How can I help you?"

"I'm here to see the front man," Ken-Yah said.

"One moment please," the robot said.

A portal opened next to Ken-Yah. She entered the portal instantly into a fancier room with antique gold, diamond, and other precious stone masks locked behind glass cases. Ken-Yah walked as she observed the golden statues around her. Fancy violin music played as she looked at the statues. She continued to walk through the room, until she reached a table. She sat down and waited patiently.

Someone appeared in front of her. He wore an elegant suit, with long straight hair sleeked back. At first, he didn't notice her, too caught up in admiring his own reflection in a mirror. "Wow, look at that handsome face." He gestured at himself in the mirror. When he noticed Ken-Yah, he got surprised.

"Ah, Ken-Yah, my favorite little firecracker. Sorry, I'm late; I was taking care of some business. How can I help you today?" he asked.

"I want a travel permit to the Sigma Galaxy. Specifically, an entry permit to Cyber Planet XYZ," she spoke.

"That can be arranged. You'll have to take part in one underground race," he replied.

"Understood," she replied.

"Great. More money for me! The next race is in five Earthian minutes. I'll need you on the track ASAP," he said as he handed her a card.

She took the card. "Cool."

A portal opened behind her, leading back to the lobby. She walked into the lobby and out the door to her space-racing car. She entered the car and brought the card to her face. A laser beam emitted from the card and scanned her eye.

A robotic voice spoke, "Racer—Ken-Yah dictated. Initiating teleportation process."

The space-racing car then disappeared and reappeared on a racetrack in a dark dome. The racetrack hovered in the air.

Suddenly, a spotlight shined down onto her and six other racers. There was no audience, only a group of rich old men that watched from a vantage point.

They had masks on and had already placed their bets.

"Gentlemen! I present to you the grand execution," the front man spoke.

A row of giant pendulum axes hung from the top of the dome down onto the racetrack.

The timer began. The racers started their engines. Go!

The racers took off. Ken-yah immediately picked up a good pace at second place. The giant pendulum axes began to swing back and forth as the racers had to dodge them. Ken-yah dodged the axes swiftly, swerving left and right according to how she needed to.

As she increased speed, bombs began to explode on random parts of the racetrack, knocking three other racers off their course. She approached a corner in which she would need to turn. Bombs exploded all around her as the pendulum axes increased the speed at which they swung. She geared in and braced herself to make the turn. As soon as she reached the corner, she executed the turn perfectly, accelerating forward in full blast.

She settled in first place with only two other racers behind her. Ahead of her, pixels began to formulate into the shape of a giant celestial wolf. The wolf began to run toward the racers, shaking the racetrack with the sheer intensity of its footsteps. The racetrack began to crumble. Ken-Yah increased the intensity at which she accelerated. She swerved and dodged the wolf. The racer in third place got caught in between its jaws.

Ken-Yah sped forward and crossed the finished line in first place.

She got out of the car and walked toward the front man who walked to her while clapping.

"Bravo." He congratulated her. "That was one of the best races my clients have watched this week." He pulled out a device and pressed a button on it.

Two entry permits materialized in Ken-Yah's hand. Sigma Galaxy entry approval.

"Thank you." She bowed politely.

"Hope your car's all right," he said as he looked behind her at the smoking car.

"I think I'll manage," she spoke.

Just then, the trunk of the car burst opened, and Sha-Nah fell out coughing and gasping for air.

Ken-Yah's eyes widened as she looked at Sha-Nah. Security showed up and pointed their guns toward them. Both girls looked frightened.

The front man rubbed his forehead in disappointment.

"Clause number 4 – Hotel Icarus Agreement—no unauthorized personnel are allowed any access to the underground events. Anybody who breaches this clause must be eliminated," the front man spoke as he checked the time on his watch.

The security guards moved closer to Ken-Yah and Sha-Nah who looked terrified. Ken-yah scanned the area for a way out. She pressed a button on her watch. A tiny portal began to form behind the car that the front man and his security could not see.

"Such a shame Ken-Yah, I had so much hope in you. Kill them both."

The security began to shoot at Ken-Yah and Sha-Nah; Ken-Yah back flipped quick enough to dodge their laser bullets, landing in her car. Sha-Nah jumped back into the passenger seat of the car. Ken-yah reversed at full speed and rushed into the portal.

The portal opened above the Icarus hotel, and Ken-Yah drove through.

Security shot at them and damaged one of the car's balancers that enabled it to retain balance in the air. The car spiraled out of control and fell downward toward the heat of the Icarus star.

Ken-Yah pressed a button on her watch, opening a portal beneath the car.

They fell into the portal and entered above the atmosphere above a cosmopolitan high-tech planet. They flew at high speed above the buildings. The car spun out of control.

Sha-Nah took control of the space-race car's controls, regaining the balance in the air.

All around them, AI in forms of robots and spatial trains flew around the city. Sha-Nah tried her best to maneuver the busy skyline and not hit any of the robots that flew past them.

A portal opened behind them.

The front man and his security were coming for them. Ken-Yah accelerated forward as Sha-Nah controlled the damaged car, making sure to dodge all machines flying by and find a safe place to land. They went at full speed forward. The car began to spark.

They desperately needed to land somewhere. Sha-Nah scanned for the nearest clear area and spotted what looked like a racing track.

Without any second thoughts, Sha-Nah raced to the track, holding the steering wheel tightly in order not to crash land. As soon as they descended upon the track, they blasted forward at maximum speed.

They crossed a finish line with a fiery acceleration. Both Ken-Yah and Sha-Nah jumped out of the car, and it exploded. They got up. They each had a ringing in their ears and a slight daze due to the rapid intergalactic travel and crash landing they had just experienced.

All around them, there was a large crowd that looked baffled. Ken-Yah rubbed her purple eyes and marveled at the sheer immensity of the coliseum they stood in. It was tall and large. The crowd stared at them, and bright lights flashed everywhere. Above them, written in holographic letters, were the words "Royal Coliseum—Cyber Planet XYZ."

It took both a while to realize what had happened. They looked up toward the screen, watching the event that had just unfolded.

It turned out that a race had started at the exact moment that Ken-Yah and Sha-Nah had descended upon the racetrack. Ken-Yah and Sha-Nah blasted forward mid race at light speed, leaving all the other three racing cars behind. So, in other words, they had blasted into a race and won it.

They looked to the racetrack, and the last racer crossed the finish line.

"Well!" a commentator spoke. "Ladies and gentlemen, it turns out that we have more than only three winners for the third round of try outs of Milky Way participants. For this round, we have an unpredicted and unexpected winning team."

Floating cameras and microphones surrounded Ken-Yah and Sha-Nah.

"So, to the unexpected victors of this race, what are your names, and what planet are you from?" the commentator asked.

A microphone came closer to Ken-Yah's face.

Someone suddenly placed a hand on her shoulder and spoke into the microphone in front of her. "The name's Ken-Yah." The front man stood behind her. "And the girl over here is…" He placed the microphone in front of Sha-Nah.

He silently whispered to Sha-Nah, "If you don't answer, I'll kill you, right here, right now."

Sha-Nah, scared, said her name into the microphone. "Sha-Nah."

The front man flashed a charming smile to the crowd. "This is Ken-Yah and Sha-Nah. From planet Earth," he spoke with confidence. "I manage them. They're under my agency."

The crowd clapped and cheered them on.

Confetti rained down as pictures were taken of them.

All the billboards in the city showcased the winners of the try-outs, with a focus on Ken-Yah and Sha-Nah's fiery entry.

Ken-Yah stood in an elevator that overlooked the high-tech cyber city.

"So, this is, the famous Cyber Planet XYZ. The most advanced planet in the Cosmos."

As she looked at the tall buildings and flying cars, the front man appeared behind her, through a portal. She saw his reflection in the glass.

"It's not my fault. I didn't know she was here," Ken-Yah said to the front man.

He lit a cigarette.

"Your little stunt cost me half my clients," he said before taking a puff and blowing out purple smoke.

"Listen Ken-Yah, the adult world is much more complex than you can imagine. I risked losing my entire business and most vital connections because of what you two girls pulled."

"Sir, in all due respect." Ken-Yah turned around to face him and looked at him straight in the eye. "She snuck into my car. I didn't know she was there."

The front man took a moment before speaking.

"You know what happens to people that put my business in danger?" he asked sternly, looking Ken-Yah right in her eyes.

Cyber City twinkled behind them, with beautiful holograms flying around.

Ken-Yah at him. "You kill them. I know." Her purple eyes glistened. "But I'm not afraid of death. I've been to the edge a lot of times. You could push me out of this elevator right now, and I'd fall smiling."

He chuckled. "You are one firecracker, aren't you?"

"You see," he spoke, "out here, no one cares about whose fault it was, all that matters is who's held accountable. I need you to win this year's Sigma Space Race. I've convinced the rest of my clients to bet on you as a retribution for my slip in confidentiality. Can you do that for me?"

"I have always wanted to compete in the Sigma Space Races, and Cyber Planet XYZ has always been calling for me. I will gladly do that. Not because I care about you, or your goddamn business." She turned around to face the Cyber City.

The front man chuckled; the elevator door opened. "You better win, Ken-Yah, your life depends on it."

He turned around to face the hallway. Ken-Yah continued looking at the city.

"Oh, and, if you need a partner, ask that girl that snuck into your car. She's got the same crazy look in her eyes that you do."

"Where is she?" Ken-Yah asked.

"Waiting at hotel esoterica with all the other racers." He stepped out; the elevator closed.

Ken-Yah took a deep breath and pressed the downward arrow on the elevator.

The elevator paused at the 22nd floor.

The door opened, and there Vaughn was. Handsome, curly hair, tall, looking hot as ever in a formal suit.

"Vaughn," she said.

"What trouble have you gotten yourself into this time?" Vaughn asked.

"It's a lot of trouble this time, I'm afraid," Ken-Yah replied.

"After you left the ISA, one of the Tuareg Sand Racers told me to give you this. She said it would be of use to you soon."

Vaughn gave Ken-Yah a glass case containing a Blue Pill. Ken-Yah took it and put it in her pocket.

"I didn't know what she meant, but now I can clearly see that you've gotten yourself into a bit of a jam," Vaughn said.

"I know, and it's only me that can get myself out of this mess," Ken-Yah replied.

"Don't get into any more trouble, okay?" he spoke.

"I'll try not to." Ken-Yah turned around and looked at Cyber City.

Vaughn placed his hands around her waist and pulled her closer to him. He leaned down and kissed her cheek. "I care about you. I don't wanna be worried all the time."

"Got it, I promise, I won't get into any more trouble," she spoke. "This was just out of my control."

He held her robot arm and kissed it. "Don't forget to oil this, okay?"

Ken-Yah nodded. A portal opened behind him, and he walked into it.

Once Ken-Yah was outside, she walked to a nearby virtual screen and clicked on the word taxi.

A taxi drove to her.

"Where to?" the robot driver asked.

"Hotel Esoterica," Ken-Yah replied and got in the car.

Hotel Esoterica:

Ken-Yah entered the large building comprising two soaring towers, moon on one end, and sun on one end. A digitalized sparkly rose window hovered above as pink pixels dropped down. A robot handed her a key with her name on it.

Ken-Yah noticed a portal with her name on it as well. She walked to the portal and entered it, instantly being transported to a lobby where her room was. She walked to the door, placed the key in. The entire room was pink and glittery. There were three beds. She figured that she'd have two other roommates.

As soon as she entered, she saw Sha-Nah sitting on the bed.

"Dude, what the hell?" Ken-Yah asked. "How did you sneak into my car?"

"Sorry," Sha-Nah explained. "I snuck into the shed because I was curious, and when you entered, I hid in the trunk, thinking that you would eventually leave. I didn't know that you would be travelling though galaxies, my bad."

"It's all right," Ken-Yah said. "Well, I'm in a bit of a jiffy. I've got to race and win. I've got to be the Sigma Space Race Champion."

"Will you be my race partner?" she asked Sha-Nah.

Sha-Nah stood up and shook Ken-Yah's hand firmly.

"You've got yourself a partner." She looked at Ken-Yah. "I won't let you down. We'll win this thing and make history."

*

"I can spontaneously combust. I can also form any gas that I want in the universe based on the atomic particles in the air around me," Sha-Nah explained to Ken-Yah as the two discussed winning strategies late in the night. "After making these rare gases, I create a combustion with them."

A flowery pink flame formed in her hand. "This is a flame formed by xenon. I have experimented with it. I've found that once injected into an engine's combustion chambers, it results in a more powerful combustion, hence, more speed. We could try with all gases creatable. This will be one of our competitive strategies. Speed."

"Yeah. Go on," Ken-Yah said.

"Our second strategy," Sha-Nah said. "Most people play it too safe in a race. We can't afford to do that, as we're rookies. We need to go all out."

"I completely agree with you on that," Ken-Yah said.

"Rookies in such a situation can't play it safe," she continued. "We need to use and try all methods possible and be as versatile as we can; we shouldn't fear anything. From what I've analyzed, you're as spontaneous as me, judging from your interdimensional racing escapades.

Also, I can analyze a race's participants and outcome in milli-seconds. This will play into our ability to change strategy at any minute."

"Yeah."

"That's our second competitive strategy. Spunk."

"Yeah, third outlast the opponents at all costs. They may have the advantage of experience, but I'm a Kaizen—stamina and endurance are two Kaizen martial art values. We must outlast everybody in this competition. Usually, when a team has both speed and spontaneity, they struggle with stamina, in that they burn out easily. We must combine these three to form a triple ark. A Triptych. Speed. Spunk. Stamina."

The two girls shook hands in a moment of power and determination. "Speed, Spunk, Stamina!"

Just then the door opened, and someone came in. It was a girl their age as them. She had bangs and straight short hair. As soon as she saw Ken-Yah and Sha-Nah, she dropped her bags and pulled out a gun, pointing it right at them. Sha-Nah and Ken-Yah both put their arms in the air.

"Woah, are you okay?" Ken-Yah asked.

"Who are you? Who sent you? Why are you in my hotel room?" the girl asked angrily as she pointed the gun at them.

"Well, I guess you didn't get the memo," Sha-Nah said. "We were put in the same room as you due to last-minute accommodation issues."

"What do you mean?" the girl asked forcefully.

"Since there were more than three winning teams in this round, one of the three rooms that were reserved needed to be shared with the fourth winner," Sha-Nah explained. "Therefore, we're your room mates."

The girl put her gun down for a moment.

"Surprise?" Ken-Yah tried to joke.

"You're the girls that blasted onto the racetrack," the girl recalled.

"Yeah," Ken-yah replied.

The girl thought for a minute, before pointing her gun at the girls once again. "If any of you try anything, I'll kill you I swear!" she yelled.

Sha-Nah leaped from the bed in the blink of an eye and knocked the gun out of the girl's hand.

The girl punched her. She punched her back. The two began to fight. Exchanging blows, punches, and kicks.

They broke glasses all over the room as they fought. Somehow, they ended up on the chandelier, swinging back and forth while still fighting.

Ken-Yah picked up the gun and pointed it toward them. They stopped and looked at her when they heard the click of the gun.

"Now we're going to do this in either one of two ways. We're all going to contain our craziness, or we'll just have to kill each other, right here in this room," Ken-Yah said.

Sha-Nah and the girl looked at each other.

Sha-Nah leaped off the chandelier and went on to unpack her bags. The other girl jumped onto her bed as well.

Ken-Yah placed the gun down. She noticed that the girl had a severe case of Fever. Her entire forehead and sides of her eyes were scorching red.

"So, I'm guessing you're from the Milky Way Galaxy as well. What planet are you from?" Ken-Yah asked.

"Planet Anhedonia," the girl said.

"Oh," Ken-Yah and Sha-Nah said simultaneously.

Planet Anhedonia was known for being the worst planet in the Milky Way Galaxy. Everything about it sucked.

"Yeah," the girl spoke. "You can judge me for being an Anhedonian, I don't care. Keep your opinions to yourself."

Sha-Nah spoke, "We didn't say anything."

"Exactly, buzz off," she said before climbing into her bed and facing the wall.

"What's your name?" Ken-Yah asked.

"Nobody," the girl spoke. "That's what you Earthians call people form Anhedonia right? I'm just a nobody, so please mind your business." She began muttering to herself. "Gosh why the flip do I have to share a room with two other people. I'll just get my trophy and go." She pulled her covers over her head. "Don't talk to me unless the hotel is burning down, or the Anti-Cosmos is attacking again. If it's none of those things, please buzz off."

Ken-Yah and Sha-Nah both sighed and fell back onto their beds, drifting off into slumber.

"These are going to be long two months," Ken-Yah said to herself as she trailed off into sleep

Chapter Four

"Today, we'll be introducing the racers from the Milky Way Galaxy who passed the tryouts." The crowd screamed excitedly.

One of Cyber Planet XYZ's high tech stadiums buzzed with life as racers from the Milky Way Galaxy prepared for their introductory event.

Ken-Yah and Sha-Nah stood in a row of race teams. Their racing car was behind them as a camera ran past them. Ken-Yah looked all around her at the large crowd and the other racers. She smiled, as above the stadium, numerous airbuses floated by. Sha-Nah's brown eyes shined with absolute bliss.

Music began to play. The crowd sang along.

Suddenly, the displays on the screens changed. A suited man appeared.

"Introducing the teams from the Milky Way Galaxy that passed the try outs and will participate in the Sigma Space Race. I'm your host, Dareth from planet Jupiter—the wettest planet in the universe."

"What?" Ken-yah pondered.

"Now, moving on to our first contestant," Dareth continued.

"Su-ha and Jake! Su-ha and Jake!" The crowd shouted, as these were their favorites.

"Su-Ha and Jake!" Dareth announced and the crowd went wild.

Ken-Yah looked over to where the team stood.

Su-ha waved around happily to the crowd. Some people in the audience sent pixelated flowers her way and lots of heart emojis.

Camera drones surrounded them as people cheered and clapped.

"Su-Ha," the host spoke. "What's on your mind for this year's Sigma Space Race?" he asked.

Su-Ha looked right into the camera and spoke, "We're going to win this thing."

Everybody cheered and went crazy at her words.

"Everyone, give it up for experienced racing team, three-time runner up, professional intergalactic team—Su-Ha and Jake!" The entire audience cheered.

"The crowd wants to know the name of your team and your racing car?" the host asked.

"This is the rocket dynamo," Su-Ha said cheerfully.

The entire crowd cheered.

The camera then moved to the second team. A tall, extremely good-looking man who looked to be around the same age as Su-ha and Jake—late 20s, early 30s—stood dressed in all leather race suit alongside a tall, beautiful woman dressed identically to him. The crowd cheered for them.

Ken-Yah and Sha-Nah stared at them in both awe and intimidation, as they knew exactly who they were. The crowd couldn't stop cheering and shouting.

"Ladies and gentlemen! The one! The only! The legendary! The phenomenal! Team spine breaker!"

The camera panned around the good-looking man and woman in a god-like moment. Ken-Yah and Sha-Nah stared wide-eyed, overcome with awe at who they were looking at.

"The Kepler 422b team won the final grand prize of the Sigma Space Race ten years ago."

The man spoke into a floating microphone. "The name's Jung," he briefly said.

"And I'm Stalliona and right here's our spine breaker," the lady said.

The crowd cheered loudly.

"Introducing the next team, E2 and E3. From Rhocancrians."

The Rhocancrians stood next to their car.

"And the next team, Gemini, and Artemis, from Venus."

The camera panned to two beautiful ladies, who smiled gracefully and waved.

"What the hell are we going to name this cat?" Sha-Nah asked.

Before Ken-Yah was done thinking of a name, the camera had reached them already.

"And here we have Sha-Nah and Ken-Yah! Two of this year's youngest racers who crashed into the try outs at lightning speed surprising everybody but eventually being accepted into the race."

A replay of how they had blasted into the racetrack showed on the screen.

"What is the name of your team?" the host asked.

"The Triptych Team," Sha-Nah said.

"Ladies and gentlemen, Ken-Yah and Sha-Nah, the Triptych Team." The crowd clapped for them.

Ken-Yah looked at Sha-Nah. "Where'd that name come from?" she asked.

"I don't even know. It was spontaneous," Sha-Nah said.

The camera moved on to the girl with bangs next. Ken-Yah and Sha-Nah's roommate. She stood at attention with an intense glare in her eyes.

The host adjusted his glasses. "Young lady, what is your name again?"

"Orion, from Anhedonia," she spoke confidently and toughly. "I do not have a racing partner. I do not believe in collaborating with another individual. I don't depend on anybody." She frowned and looked straight ahead.

"Okay, ladies and gentlemen, the final participant from the Milky Way Galaxy, Orion from Anhedonia!"

"Now, we'll be announcing the only racers from the Sigma Galaxy," the announcer said.

"First." The camera panned to two good-looking twins with long hair. The crowd cheered before the announcer spoke. "The prettiest racers in the Cosmos. Levi and fletcher from Cyber Planet XYZ."

Levi and fletcher smiled, everyone swooned because of their good looks. The announcer moved on.

"Right next to them are Ni-Ki and Ki-Ra from the Shinto Galaxy."

Race One – Inteplanetary

Ken-Yah and Sha-Nah sat in their car, eyes steady and staring straight at the road. The other racers were Jung and Stallioná, Su-Ha and Jake, and Fletcher and Levi. The Rhocancrians E2 and E3. Gemini and Artemis from Venus. Team Pluto. And Orion. The crowd watched in anticipation.

Ready. Set. Go!

A canon was blasted into the air. The cars drifted off in their separate lanes. Ken-Yah pressed down on the acceleration, but she and Sha-Nah trailed behind in last place. Orion took first place immediately; her racing skills were quick and agile. The race continued; Su-Ha and Jake's car shot up into the air and flew past Orion at full speed. Orion fell into third place, being overtaken by Jung and Stallioná as well. Team Pluto took fourth place. Team Space Dust tied in fifth place with the Rhocancrians. Gemini and Artemis took sixth place. Ken-Yah and Sha-Nah still in last place.

Ken-Yah noticed that a corner was ahead. She smiled. "Perfect." She twisted the wheels and the back tires of the car turned. "Now!" she yelled.

Sha-Nah released a fiery ball of a red flame into the car's combustion chamber, blasting them forward at full speed. They passed the Rhocancrians, Team Space Dust, Gemini and Artemis, Team Pluto and caught up to tie with Orion in third place. They got closer to the finish line. Ken-Yah stepped harder on the accelerator. The car went super-fast that it left sparks behind it.

They finished the race tied with Orion at third place. Su-ha and Jake were in first place, Jung and Stallioná in second place. Team Space Dust were fourth, the Rhocancrians were fifth, Team Pluto sixth, Gemini and Artemis finished seventh, and Team Rania last.

"Coming in third, Orion from Planet Anhedonia." The crowd cheered as Orion advanced to get her trophy. "In second place, Jung and Stallioná." The crowd cheered once again as Team Spine Breaker advanced to their trophy. "And in first place, Team Su-Ha! And Jake." The crowd went wild at the mention of their names as they took the 1st place trophy.

"And now that we have our three winners for this round," the mc spoke, "let us count the points earned in the race to see which three other teams get to move on to the next round." A ballot counted the votes.

Ken-Yah and Sha-Nah looked at the numbers in anticipation.

"Team Pluto – 69 points, Team Rania – 40 points, Gemini and Artemis – 30 points, Rhocancrians – 50 points, Fletcher and Levi – 89 points, and Ken-Yah and Sha-Nah – 80 points," the host spoke. "According to the rules of the

Sigma Space Races, only the teams that score 80 and above points get to proceed on merit."

"Yes!" Ken-Yah and Sha-Nah high fived each other. They were to proceed to the next level on merit along with team milky.

Race Two – Interplanetary Quarter

Sha-Nah and Ken-Yah suited up. Zipping up their costumes, they made their way through a hallway with their game faces on. They looked at each other and nodded. For race two of the interplanetary quarter, the racetrack flew over the city all the way above a large body of water beyond the buildings.

They entered their racecar. Ken-Yah took hold of the wheels and turned on the engines. The car rumbled as the wheels got ready for take-off. As soon as the whistle blew, they sped off. Sha-Nah in the next seat placed her hand into the transmuter to send firepower to the engines. They car blasted ahead at full speed. Ken-Yah determinedly stepped on the acceleration and controlled the navigations. They were in second place.

They drove above the city buildings and, eventually, over the water body. Ken-Yah's heartbeat fast, but that is what she loved, the thrill of it all. As they came into a corner, she accidentally did not turn in time. The car flew off the racetrack. However, Sha-Nah blasted more into the exhaust system enough to change the car's trajectory back onto the racetrack. The car bounced and got back to driving at fast speed. They were now in the last place. Orion was just ahead of them. They kept a steady acceleration as they caught up to Orion, who seemed to be struggling with something inside her racecar.

Suddenly, a lever on the side of Orion's car exploded. Her car drifted off the racetrack and fell into the lake below. Ken-Yah and Sha-Nah's car was still speeding.

"I'll check on her," Sha-Nah said as she flew out of the window and used her combustion powers to create a turbo force under her feet and propel her forward. She headed to Orion's sinking car. Sha-Nah held Orion's hand and flew back to the racetrack with her.

"Thanks," Orion said.

Sha-Nah was in too much of a haste to reply. She flew directly to the racing car; the two jumped in through the window, joining Ken-Yah inside. Orion sat in the back seat and Sha-Nah settled in the passenger seat where she handled the controls to prepare for another combustion blast. They were now in third place, as Ken-Yah concentrated on catching up with the racer in second place. Sha-Nah shot fire into the transmitter, and the car blasted forward, taking second place. The girls laughed in excitement as the sudden speed exhilarated them. They were now head-to-head, tied with Su-Ha and Jake.

"Woah, this ought to be interesting. A tie between Su-ha and Jake with Ken-Yah and Sha-Nah, as the two persistently race for first place," the commentator spoke.

Suddenly, there was a problem with their racecar, the exhaust pipe began to make a sound. The car began to malfunction and fall behind, as explosions emitted from the exhaust pipe.

"Something's stuck in the exhaust pipe," Ken-Yah shouted as the controls showed red signs of danger. "The car's going to blow up. We'll have to jump out."

"I'll get it," Orion said before climbing out of the car, to the trunk to lean over the exhaust pipe. She reached into it and took out a device. She looked at the device; it had an encryption on it. The care began to move steadily. Orion jumped back in.

Sha-Nah shot fire into the transmitter once again, and the car blasted forward, catching back up to their opponents.

Su-ha looked at Ken-Yah, Sha-Nah, and Orion from the driver's seat.

She smiled at them and waved.

They waved back and smiled as well.

"*Adios*, haha!" Su-ha said before her RACE CAR blasted forward. The three girls looked forward in shock at Su-ha's sudden speed.

Ken-Yah, Sha-Nah, and Orion looked at each other and looked back at the racetrack ahead with mischievous faces. Suddenly, they all shouted. "Speed! Spunk! Stamina!"

Sha-Nah blasted more fire into the transmitter and ken-yah pressed harder on the accelerator. They sped forward and caught up to Su-ha and Jake. Ken-Yah smiled at Su-ha, who was visibly shocked.

"*Hasta la vista!* Baby!" Ken-Yah shot forward and crossed first place within thirty seconds.

The crowd cheered as the girls rested back in their seats and smiled at each other. "We did it girls," Sha-nah squealed. "Our first win and we beat two racing champions. I can't believe it!"

They got out of the car. "Ken-Yah! Sha-Nah! Orion! Ken-Yah! Sha-Nah! Orion!" The crowd cheered their names.

The three girls made their way up to the podium, where they were to receive their trophy. They were handed flowers by robot drones as cameras surrounded them.

"Is your team officially a trio?" a lady asked them.

The girls looked at each other.

"Yes," Ken-Yah said. "We're a trio."

"Everybody give it up for our winning trio, Ken-Yah, Orion, and Sha-Nah," the commentator spoke.

Everybody cheered. Ken-yah was handed the trophy as the podium rose slightly up into the air for the audience to get a clear view of them. Confetti rained down on them.

Next to them on the podium were six other teams from different galaxies. Among them were Fletcher and Levi for the Sigma Galaxy, plus Ni-ki and Ki-ra for the Shinto Galaxy.

Sha-Nah was having the time of her life. She smiled, laughed, cheered, and danced, enjoying all the praise of the crowd.

"Oh, thank you! Thank you!" She blew kisses to the audience. "I've never had this much attention before." She squealed, "This is so exciting! Ahhhh!" Sha-Nah danced around heartily.

Ken-Yah stared straight ahead, with a deadly and fiery look in her eyes. She looked around her; she spotted her image in the big screen.

The crowd then began to cheer her name, "Ken-Yah! Ken-Yah! Ken-Yah!" She looked back at the trophy in her hands, then straight ahead into the cameras again.

Ken-Yah had a drive in her eyes as she looked directly at the camera.

That night, Ken-Yah walked out of Hotel Esoterica, walked to a building a short distance away. The door opened for her, and she entered a high-tech lab.

Vaughn and Santino had assembled a team of the best technicians from Vaporwave City to build an effective car for Ken-Yah.

Vaughn walked to Ken-Yah and hugged her.

"You're just in time; we just finished updating your new car. Here it is," Santino said as he unveiled the car to Ken-Yah.

Ken-Yah walked around the car as she admired it. "It's amazing," she said.

Vaughn smiled. "Not only that, but there's also this." He pressed a button on a remote, and an advanced racing suit came down from above. Equipped with its own mask, and gloves. The suit was called 'Star Hero.'

"It's a custom-made racing suit, designed for you," Vaughn said. "It's equipped with shock absorbers, the ability to climb walls, anti-gravity mechanisms, and many more functions you need to win this race."

"Woah," Ken-Yah said as she touched the suit.

Vaughn pressed the finger of the suit. It turned into a ring.

"The entire suit is stored in this ring." He showed the ring to Ken-Yah and put it on her finger.

Vaughn said, "And look." He took a key and handed it to Ken-Yah.

"What is that?" Ken-Yah asked.

"It's called Midnight," Vaughn replied.

Vaughn pressed the key, and a purple-eyed black panther appeared in front of Ken-Yah.

Ken-Yah was impressed.

He pressed the key again, and the purple-eyed panther turned into a motorcycle.

"This is really cool," Ken-Yah said and climbed onto the motorcycle.

She pressed the ring on her finger and activated her racing suit. She tested the engines of the motorcycle.

Vaughn put on his helmet and got on his motorcycle as well.

"You read my mind," Ken-Yah said.

The door opened. Vaughn and Ken-Yah rode out of the lab. They rode throughout Cyber City, passing by the bright highways, with the beautiful buildings and holograms in the distance.

*

Ken-Yah returned back to Hotel Esoterica after riding through Cyber City and found Sha-Nah and Orion were preparing for the next race. The three girls set up a hologram and began to plan.

Suddenly, someone broke into their hotel room through their window. The girls were startled.

It was a tall guy in a military suit and mask. He pointed his gun at them. They froze in fear.

Then, he flipped Ken-Yah's bed over.

Below Ken-Yah's bed was a tiny device that was counting down to something.

He picked up the device and threw it out of the window. It exploded in the air.

The girls were so confused. It looked as though someone had planted a bomb under Ken-Yah's bed.

Just then, someone kicked the door open. Levi and Fletcher ran into the room. They were holding swords, and they looked like they had just been fighting outside.

"Did you stop the bomb?" Levi asked.

"I did," the military guy replied.

He took off his mask, revealing a handsome face. "I'm Divus, commander of the Intergalactic Military. I have reason to believe that someone has intentions to sabotage this year's Sigma Space Races. And that person is specifically after you," He pointed at Ken-Yah.

"Me?" she asked. "Why?"

"We have intel that this person placed a large bet on one of the teams. However, they are afraid that you might ruin their chances and make them lose billions. There's a target on your back," Commander Divus said.

"What?" Sha-Nah's eyes widened with shock.

Ken-Yah said, "I don't think it's that serious. I'm just a teenage girl; I can't pose much of a threat."

"Ken-Yah," Commander Divus said, "I don't mean to frighten you, but someone is coming to kill you. They've assembled a team of mercenaries. They have a bounty on your head. All the crooks in the city have been sent to hunt the dark-skinned girl with the purple eyes."

Ken-Yah looked at Commander Divus as the realization dawned on her.

"The Intergalactic Military has appointed Levi and Fletcher as undercover guards. They are members of Cyber Planet XYZ's fleet of knights," Commander Divus said. "They shall be in charge of your safety until we get to the bottom of this."

Commander Divus walked to the window. His car flew to the building. Before he left, he handed communication devices to Ken-Yah, Sha-Nah, and Orion. "When you are in trouble, use these devices to contact either me or Levi and Fletcher all right?"

The girls nodded.

He got into his car and flew away.

Ken-Yah, Sha-Nah, and Orion looked at each other. Then, they looked at Levi and Fletcher. Fletcher used a building device to fix the window and the door. Then, he placed an alarm at the door.

"If you guy need any help, call us," Levi said.

Intergalactic Races – First Race

Ken-Yah adjusted the gears by her side. Sha-Nah input instructions into the navigation manual as Orion sat in the backseat reading a virtual map. Ready! Set! Go!

The car sped off at maximum capacity. There were seven other racers on the track. Ken-Yah concentrated her eyes onto the track as she had a dead shot look in her eyes. The speed was exhilarating. The racetrack reached far above the city clouds, at a point where the sun and the moon could be seen. They were to finish the race at the two tallest towers in the city named Jachin and Boaz that stood right under the two celestial bodies, the highest points peaking above the clouds. The racetrack had a little bit of static due to the electric current of the clouds and the unique magnetic field of Cyber Planet XYZ.

"The static on the racetrack seems to be creating sparks, making it tougher for the racers to reach the two towers of Jachin and Boaz," the commentator spoke.

Ken-Yah smiled as explosions happened all around her. Sha-Nah laughed in delight.

"Left. Right. Left." Orion's map showed where the explosions would happen and read out what direction Ken-Yah had to turn.

Ken-Yah swerved accordingly.

"One of the Ken-Yah's special tactics is the agility at which she can swerve accurately at any moment without drifting off the racetrack."

Ken-Yah continued to swerve left and right.

Above them, a meteor shower began to run across the sky; it was multi-colored and pretty.

Sha-Nah lit the transmuter with an orange flame, causing the car to shoot forward and take second place.

They approached the twin towers of Jachin and Boaz. The towers were purple in color and lit with neon lights at the top. The girls felt excited as they approached the finish line that was in between the two towers. They directly tied with Su-Ha and Jake, as well as Ni-ki and Ki-ra, and Fletcher and Levi. The four teams crossed the finished line at the same time. A picture was taken at the exact moment of crossing.

"It looks like we have a tie of three teams." The crowd cheered.

The four other teams crossed the finish line shortly after.

Ken-Yah, Sha-Nah, Orion, Su-ha, Jake, Ni-ki, Ki-ra, Fletcher, and Levi hovered in the air.

"Folks, you know what this means, we'll need a follow up race to find the exact first, second, and third place. In an iconic race to the death." The crowd cheered.

"Yes!" Su-ha cheered excitedly.

Fletcher and Levi looked shocked.

Ken-Yah smiled as she looked at Ken-Yah and Orion. "Speed! Spunk! Stamina!" They screamed and hit their fists together.

"Let's win this thing!"

"Yeah!"

Ken-Yah held the steering wheel and smiled excitedly as her eyes glimmered.

"The racers will have to race through the danger zone in the orbit of the Sigma Star. The star that powers up Cyber Planet XYZ."

The racers looked up. The Sigma Star was a long distance above Cyber Planet XYZ and radiated large amounts of lethal rays. A racetrack formed from where they were all the way up to the star. Ready! Set! Go!

The racers drove upward toward the star. Orion climbed outside of the car, one handheld the window ledge as she hung by the arm, staring upward at the star. Taking out a gadget, she held it close to her eye and read a few codes that appeared on it, before jumping back into the car.

"The radiation level is quite high today," she said to Ken-Yah and Sha-Nah.

"Sha-Nah, can you harness the star's energy to give us more combustion power?" Ken-Yah asked.

Sha-Nah held her hand out of the window. A ball of gas formed in her hand. She put her hand back into the car and formed a silver flame with that gas. "I'm not sure if this chemical reaction will either make us win or blow us to bits," she said to Ken-Yah.

"What should we do?" Orion asked ken-yah.

Ken-Yah smiled. "That's why we call it spontaneity baby." She grinned. "Put it in."

Sha-Nah blasted the gas into the combustor.

The exhaust pipe let out a bright white flame with a loud blasting sound that shot them forward miles ahead of the other racers. The girls laughed as the blast propelled them at a speed they had never felt before. Before they knew it, the car had lifted off the racetrack all the way to right in front of the Sigma Star.

The Sigma Star was a bright ball of gas. Time stopped in that moment, as they looked right at the Sigma Star. They were in awe. The moment was short lived when the car dropped back down onto the racetrack. Ken-Yah stepped on the acceleration and shot forward as Sha-Nah and Orion held on tight to their seats.

Neon lights flew past them, as they got closer to Su-Ha and Jake who were in first place. They sped past them and crossed the finish line in no time.

Leaning back in their seats, they let-out sighs of relief and hi-fived each other in excitement.

Ken-Yah, Sha-Nah, Orion in first place, Su-Ha and Jake in second place, and Felix and Levi in fourth place. In fifth place were Jachin and Boaz, representing Cyber Planet XYZ. And in sixth place, Ni-ki and Ki-ra.

Race Two – Intergalactic

"For race two of the intergalactic round, the racetrack spirals above the Sigma Star in a circular motion, giving the racers a total of six rounds to race. However, the radiation emitted by the star risks melting the tires of the racers. How will they do this? Watch to find out," the host spoke as the racers concentrated.

Ready. Set. Go!

The racers took off, Ken-Yah, Sha-Nah and Orion taking the lead in the first round. The crowd cheered for them.

"Ladies and gentlemen, in the lead, we have the Triptych Team, followed closely by Su-ha and Jake, then Fletcher and Levi!"

The second round passed, in the third round, the Triptych Team's car began to slow down, making them trail behind.

"Oh no, we don't have enough combustion power," Sha-Nah said. "Even if I make a flame, it will not be able to react if we have no combustion power."

Orion grabbed her katana sword from under the chair. She climbed outside the window of the car.

"What are you doing?" Ken-yah asked.

"My katana is made from a special kind of material that can turn high levels of radiation into horsepower. It's this way because Planet Anhedonia has high levels of radiation. We learn at a very young age how to use this material to convert radiation into kinetic energy," she spoke.

"But you don't know what kind of radiation the Sigma Star emits; this isn't the Milky Way after all. One wrong move, and you could perish," Sha-Nah said, concerned.

"Me, perish?" Orion laughed as she hovered outside the car. "Just who the hell do you think I am?" She smirked before leaping off the racetrack and descending downward to the Sigma Star. She had a determined look on her face as she shot downward right to it. She raised her katana, ready to make an impact. She shot into the star making way right to its core. As soon an impact was made, there was a blast that emitted from the star.

Orion then shot right out, with a trail of radiation from the star, connecting to her katana. She then aimed her katana at the Triptych Team's car and blasted the radiation power to the car. The car was instantly powered up; the horsepower rose beyond maximum and even burned the meter that was measuring it, with a bright purple flame.

"Ha! Team Triptych world domination!" Orion shouted as she flew back to the car and held on to the window.

The car went too fast and ended up rising off the racetrack. It began to spin as it left a trailed of fire behind. "Ahh!" the girls screamed, as they held on tight.

The car blasted past the finish line and crash-landed. The girls jumped out.

"Yeah!" They high fived each other "Speed! Spunk! Stamina!" they shouted.

The car exploded behind them, disintegrating into pieces, and setting on fire.

The girls looked at the burning car. Ken-Yah laughed. Sha-Nah and Orion laughed as well.

Fletcher and Levi ran to them.

"Are you guys all right?" Fletcher asked.

"Yeah," Ken-Yah replied.

"Good job," Levi said,

"Thanks," the girls replied.

There was another explosion once again, and the entire car dissipated into ash.

Portals formed all around them, and reporters flooded on the racetrack to take pictures of the girls and interview them. There was chaos all over the racetrack.

A cute girl with the brightest smile stood in front of a camera as she spoke, "Reporting live for the Andromeda Galaxy teen news, and this is Evora, all the way from the orbit of the Sigma Star in the Sigma Galaxy. We have just finished watching what many are describing as one of the most iconic races in the history of Sigma Space Racing. Right now, I'm going to interview the star racers from the Milky Way Galaxy." She walked to Ken-Yah.

"Hi Ken-Yah, I'm Evora from the Andromeda Galaxy teen news. Could I interview you for a minute?" she asked.

"Sure," Ken-Yah replied.

"So, are your hopes high after winning two matches in a row?" Evora asked.

"Well, my sporting blood is up. I'm ready to face any situation, that's all I can tell you," Ken-Yah said.

"Can I request for a picture of the three of you?" Evora asked. "Levi and Fletcher, could you join the picture if you don't mind?"

"Sure, no problem," Fletcher said.

They posed in front of Fletcher and Levi's car. The Triptych Team stood at the front as the twins stood at the side. Little did they know that that would become one of the most memorable pictures of their lives.

Just then, Ken-Yah got a notification on her watch. It was a message from Princess Starlight of Solaris. The message was delivered in the format of a hologram. It read, "Nice work on the race today. Hit me up when you're free."

Ken-Yah looked at Orion and Sha-Nah. "How do you guys feel about an Adventure on Solaris?" she asked.

Sha-Nah's eyes widened. "I've always wanted to go to Solaris," she said.

"Me too," Orion said. "So what's the plan?"

"Well…" Ken-Yah smirked.

Next thing, the girls were speed racing on dirt bikes through the desert planet Solaris. Giant Pyramids surrounded them, built by a species of giants on Solaris known as the Annunaki, who also protected the central palace of the planet.

Ken-Yah, Sha-Nah, and Orion were speeding past the pyramids on motorcycles, with helmets on. One of the Solaris suns shone in the distance.

As they approached Solaria—the capital, they were stopped by the Solaris Royal Guard who held advanced golden spears created by the mineral that made Solaris other most military efficient planet in the Cosmos.

"State your name and your business," the lead guard said. She widened her eyes, and they flowed a sharp golden color.

Ken-Yah took off her helmet.

"Ken-Yah. Princess Starlight's friend," she said, her purple eyes gleamed.

The guards moved aside instantly.

"Ms. Ken-Yah, of course, the princess told us she's expecting you," the lead guard said. "Unfortunately, only you will be allowed to see the princess. But we shall show your friends to the guests resort, where they will be very comfortable."

Ken-Yah looked at Sha-Nah and Orion to see if they were okay with that.

They nodded yes.

"Should we escort you to the royal pyramid?" the lead guard asked.

"Nah, it's okay," Ken-Yah said as she stepped off the bike. "I know my way around."

Ken-Yah walked through Solaris to the central pyramid. It was tall, with a glowing blue top. The glowing blue top was the secret to Solaris's military power. But nobody in the Cosmos knew what was up there.

She entered the Royal pyramid, walked to the tech area, and found Princess Starlight working on a portal.

Princess Starlight was concentrating on a bunch of equations. She turned and saw Ken-Yah; a smile immediately appeared on her face. Such a beautiful princess with curly pretty hair. It was always a delight meeting her.

"Ken-Yah," Princess Starlight said. "What a wonderful surprise!"

She walked to Ken-Yah and hugged her. Ken-Yah was just like a little sister to her.

"How are you? I see you're killing it in the Sigma Space Races, I gotta admit, I thought you'd finish high school first," she said as she played with Ken-Yah's hair.

"Screw school," Ken-Yah said, "I hate it."

Princess Starlight gave Ken-Yah a reprimanding look.

Ken-Yah quickly corrected herself. "I mean, I am willing to be patient with school and finally do what I love when I graduate."

"That's better." Princess Starlight chuckled.

"What are you working on?" Ken-Yah asked, as she looked at the machine that Princess Starlight was working on.

"We're trying to make a portal to a certain point in time and space. It seems to have deleted itself from the space time continuum," Princess Starlight said.

"Hey, let's take a selfie," Princess Starlight said as she held her phone. Ken-Yah posed for the picture.

"Mind if I post it?" Princess Starlight asked.

"I don't mind at all," Ken-Yah replied.

Princess Starlight posted the picture to her billions of followers online and immediately they went crazy, seeing the Princess and the racing star together.

Just then, two girls entered the tech lab.

"Yes, girls," Princess Starlight said. "Any news?"

"We just returned from Earth 1. The king of Hyperborea still won't talk to the DVF. And he's still keeping the red haired girl hostage," one of the twins said.

"Thank you girls, you may go," Princess Starlight said.

They left the lab.

"What were they talking about?" Ken-Yah asked.

"Just some Solaris political affairs," Princess Starlight said. "Although, knowing how explosive you are, I think you might get involved in Solaris affairs pretty soon." She chuckled.

"Oh, that reminds me," Ken-Yah said. "Do you have any racing cars I can borrow? Mine blew up."

Chapter Five

Princess Starlight gave the girls an advanced 444-model space-racing car. Way more advanced than the previous 333 model.

They spent all night in the training facility, working diligently with all their will, to renovate it according to how they wanted it.

At dawn, they looked at the car. It looked powerful. Strong rims, engine, tires, wheels, and a larger combustion chamber.

"Attention all racers, race three of the intergalactic quarter begins in fifteen minutes. You are all required to make your way to the cyber city coliseum, where you will be transported to the venue of the race."

"Let's go Team Triptych," Ken-Yah said, raising her fist in the air.

Race Three – Intergalactic:

The racetrack was just outside of the Tómr planet. The Triptych Team raced against the other teams from other galaxies. They trailed in the middle position as they passed countless corners, for the racetrack was a spiral.

The racetrack, however, had random explosions in random areas; this was done to increase the difficulty of the race. Many racers were knocked off the track and went flying off into space.

Sha-Nah created different flames and blasted them into the combustion chamber. Ken-Yah tactfully dodged all the explosions and maneuvered in the most efficient way through the racetrack.

Orion sat on top of the car in a meditative position, perfectly still and unshaken, despite all the explosions happening around her. "I spy with my little eye, an idiot that's about to die," she said to herself. The racer in front of them got caught up in an explosion, and his car disintegrated.

The Triptych Team reached second position. With Su-Ha and Jake in the first position, but ahead of them by a large distance. They closed in on them, getting nearer and nearer.

Until suddenly, a large beast fell from above. It shook the whole racetrack. Ken-Yah raised an eyebrow.

"What the?"

"What the heck is that?" Sha-Nah looked at the large monster in front of them.

The giant Minotaur walked around the racetrack in a confused manner, kicking cars off the track and roaring. When it spotted Ken-Yah, it began to run to the Triptych Team's car.

Orion drew her katana sword and leaped into the air.

"Hey, ugly," she called.

"Stop interrupting our grinding." Orion kicked the monster in the face, making it stumble back a bit.

The monster swung its large hand at her. With one swipe of her sword, she cut its arm. She then proceeded to sidekick the monster across the face. It fell off the racetrack. She then flew back to the Triptych Team and sat on top of the car.

They got closer to the first position. However, they were interrupted when a large rock hit their car and steered them off the racetrack.

They went spinning into space as they screamed. Ken-Yah gained control of the car's momentum and shot back onto the racetrack once again.

They looked all around them. Large rocks big enough to crush them like ants fell down onto the racetrack. Ken-Yah dodged them with utmost precision as she stepped harder on the acceleration. They got closer to Su-Ha and Jake, eventually passing them, and gaining first place.

*

"The rocks stopped falling as we got closer to Su-Ha and Jake," Ken-Yah said to Sha-Nah and Orion. "That means the rocks were put there to sabotage us. And the monster too."

"I'm suspecting that whoever is sabotaging these races is affiliated with Su-Ha and Jake," Ken-Yah added.

The Triptych Team walked into a lobby where the other racers waited for a press conference that would involve Cyber Planet XYZ officials and the racers; Ken-Yah noticed that none of the racers wanted to stand next to them. She locked eyes with Su-Ha for a second before Su-Ha frowned and looked away. Every other team was chatting casually with other racers, leaving the Triptych Team out.

They were being othered.

"We're not wanted here," Ken-Yah said to Sha-Nah and Orion.

During the press conference, interviewers asked the racers questions team by team. When it was the Triptych Team's turn, everyone went silent.

"My question for the Triptych Team is," one interviewer spoke, "everyone says that you do not deserve to be in this race, and all your winnings so far have been out of pure luck and chance. What do you have to say about this?"

The girls looked at each other.

Ken-Yah then spoke up. "Listen to me," she said, "you might try to intimidate us, and make us believe that we don't belong here."

Orion pulled out a book from her bag and handed it to Ken-Yah.

"But clause five of the Intergalactic Sports Agreement states that equal opportunity shall be granted to anyone that wishes to participate in a competition," Ken-Yah said as she showed clause five to the interviewer.

The Triptych Team got up.

"Let this be known," Ken-Yah said. "The Triptych Team folds to no one."

Ken-Yah walked out. Sha-Nah and Orion followed her. Paparazzi took pictures of them as they walked out. That night, Ken-Yah went viral on the internet; "Leader of Triptych Team responds rudely to press."

Race Four – Intergalactic

Ready! Set! Go!

The racers took off. This time the race was in the fluorescent solar system, a system of beautiful neon lights and patterns. The Triptych Team raced diligently, tying with Fletcher and Levi at third place, with Su-Ha and Jake in first place, and Ni-ki and Ki-ra in second place. The Triptych Team then trailed behind into fifth place as two other racers passed them.

The Triptych Team slowed down and settled in last place.

"Ladies and gentlemen!" the host spoke in the coliseum. "It appears that the Triptych Team has slowed down. Well, all the comments and concerns might have been right; perhaps they are not legible or experienced enough to participate in the Sigma Space Races."

Boooo!

The crowd began to degrade the Triptych Team.

Ken-Yah slowed down even more until she stopped the car completely.

The car was parked. No motion at all, as the other racers continued ahead. Time was going; the race would soon end.

The Triptych Team was left behind by miles. A camera flew to the car, showcasing to the audience what was happening.

The entire coliseum went silent as Ken-Yah stepped out of the car.

Ken-Yah walked to the front of the car and looked straight into the camera. She tilted her head a bit before making a gun sign with her two fingers toward her head.

As though she was pointing a real gun toward her head. The entire audience all over the Cosmos watched in confusion as to what was happening. She then turned her hand to the camera to look like she was pointing a gun at the audience. And with a shooting motion she whispered… "Bang!"

Suddenly, the Triptych Team's car transformed. With sparks of fire, metal arms, legs, and gadgets emerged from the car, turning it into a large mecha robot. The entire audience was speechless.

"Woah!" the host said. "It looks the Triptych Team's car has transformed into a mecha robot. And not just any mecha robot, this is more advanced than any I've ever seen. And not just any mecha robot, one of the most advanced military robots I have ever seen."

"That's some Solaris type of military technology right there. Could take out the Intergalactic military," the other host said.

Ken-Yah smiled and leaped into the air. She flew into the pilot seat in the forehead of the robot. Orion and Sha-Nah sat at the pilot seats in the eyes of the robot.

"And that's the super Triptych mega robot! Speed! Spunk stamina!" Ken-Yah shouted.

"Speed! Spunk! Stamina!" Orion and Sha-Nah shouted.

Ken-Yah handled the controls and the mecha robot leaped into the air and flew ahead, with fire blasting out of the engines on its back. They caught up to the other teams in seconds.

The mecha robot landed, and wheels came out underneath its feet. The mecha robot began to skate in its lane past the other racers, who just looked on in shock.

The robot then transformed back into a car, and the Triptych Team finished first.

The girls won once again.

Their happiness was short lived. The next day, the press released multiple articles about the fact that the girls did not earn their win fairly.

"A thing such as the renovation of a car has never been seen before in the history of the Sigma Space Races; therefore, the Triptych Team must meet the Sigma Galaxy Officials to defend their right to continue with the race. Otherwise, the collective agrees that they do not deserve a shot at the trophy due to their immature and spontaneous nature."

Ken-Yah and Sha-Nah watched a news broadcast from the hotel room.

Hordes of rioters took to the streets outside Hotel Esoterica. Some were gamblers who had lost their money betting on other teams, and some were die-hard fans of the sport who thought that a bunch of inexperienced teenage girls did not deserve any opportunities to win.

"Eliminate the Triptych team! Eliminate the Triptych Team!" The crowd yelled.

"Excuse me, sir, could you tell us why you're here today?" Evora, the reporter from Andromeda News, asked one of the rioters.

"I'm here to advocate for the disqualification of team Triptych, because I believe the Sigma Space Race Tournament is something serious and that real worthy participants should be allowed to race, not just any inexperienced contender."

Suddenly, the man was interrupted when Orion came running outside, with two num-chuks in her hand. She hit his head with one num-chuk causing him to faint on the spot. She ran toward the rest of the crowd who got scared and ran away.

Orion then walked to Evora and asked for the microphone. Evora gave her the microphone. She looked into the camera.

"Listen to me, you chumps who think me and my girls don't deserve a shot at the trophy. Do you see these?" She gave the microphone back to Evora and raised her num-chuks. "These can turn into any weapon in the universe." She applied pressure to them, and they turned into katana swords.

"I can stab you with a sword; I can hit you with a baseball bat." The swords turned into baseball bats. "And my favorite." The baseball bats turned into iron gloves around Orion's fists. "Iron fist boxing gloves that can knock you out or kill you in a second. So, if you keep talking jive, you'll go down in five. I'll fight all of you and punch you into the Anti-Cosmos. Anyone who has something to say, come say it now. I'm giving you five minutes. Get down here to Hotel Esoterica, and we'll settle this fist to fist."

Sha-Nah's mouth dropped in disbelief. "Orion's lost it."

Ken-Yah got up and walked out of the hotel room; Sha-Nah followed her.

Orion turned to Evora. "You saw how they ran?"

Evora nodded.

"They knew they wanted no piece of me, or these fists. I've got a knockout power harder than any stone or metal in the Cosmos," Orion said.

The next day, the girls were called to face the Sigma Galaxy Officials to defend their right to the trophy.

The hearing took place in a large hall, filled with guests, a jury, and a judge.

"Do you girls have anything to say for yourselves?" the judge asked.

Ken-Yah began to speak. "You all say that we do not deserve a shot because we are inexperienced and that our performance in the last race was too spontaneous right? Well let me ask you this. Did you start the Sigma Space

Race Tournament so you could push a bunch of old racers and bore the audience? Because when I read about the Sigma Space Race, I read that it was a cosmic-wide event that sought to bring all the Cosmos together in one big action packed and entertaining showcase. But instead of bringing the Cosmos together, you're insisting on gatekeeping the event due to prejudice, and in turn, boring the entire universe while you are at it. So, I tell you this sir, you asked us what we have to say for ourselves, now I will ask you what you have to say for yourself. Do you intend for the Sigma Space Race to be a discriminatory and ageist sport? Tell us now, while the whole universe is watching so that everybody can get a valid picture of what the Sigma Space Race really is."

The entire audience looked at the officials. There was dead silence in the hall. All the cameras pointed at the old man judge, curious as to what he was going to say. Something in his eyes glimmered as he looked at the Triptych Team. They looked back at him with determined eyes.

"Case overruled," he spoke before getting up. "The Triptych Team is free to race." He made his way out of the hall.

*

The Triptych Team got back to Hotel Esoterica and hung out on the rooftop.

Overlooking the Cyber City, as they watched the sunset. They ran across the buildings tall buildings of Cyber City, jumping from one rooftop to another.

When they finally settled on one rooftop with the high-tech city all around them, Sha-Nah took out her phone and opened her internet profile. There were millions of notifications. After the first intergalactic race, the three girls had become overnight sensations across every metaverse pocket of the internet. They were being looked up from every search engine and social site in every galaxy.

Even though conventional space racing fans had not embraced them, most people were being drawn to them due to their charisma, and they had in fact brought in more new viewers than ever. Their faces were everywhere, on every corner of the cosmic internet.

Sha-Nah's social profile flooded with hearts and follows.

Ken-Yah pulled out her phone and checked hers. It was the same thing. The girls read the comments. It was such a surprise to them that they had gone viral.

"They found my profile, and I don't even have a picture up…" Orion laughed.

The girls scrolled through their social feeds reading all the messages and chats from their fans.

Sha-Nah's phone beeped with a sign, "Recommended: go live now to chat with your followers."

Sha-Nah pressed the live button and the camera opened. Hearts filled the side of her screen as her followers logged on and left numerous comments.

"Hi, I'm Sha-Nah."

"I'm Orion."

"I'm Ken-Yah."

"And we are," Ken-Yah said.

"Team Triptych."

They continued the live stream, talking to their fans until they were back in their hotel room.

"I've got this egg. My friend gave it to me," Orion said before pulling an egg out of her pocket and showing it to the camera.

"An egg," Ken-Yah asked surprised. "Where'd you get your egg from?"

"My friend from the cafeteria gave it to me, she was like you expound too much energy for such a tiny person, and here you need some protein."

"Out of nowhere?" Sha-Nah asked.

"Yeah." Orion looked at her. "Out of nowhere."

Sha-Nah continued reading the comments on their live. Ken-Yah asked for the egg and Orion gave it to her, but in the process, it fell onto the floor. The three girls paused.

"It fell, omg."

"Oh, it fell." Ken-Yah looked down. "Where did it go?"

"It rolled over there." Sha-Nah walked to a corner to pick up the egg.

"Thank goodness, it's not raw," Orion said.

"Are you sure?" Sha-Nah asked.

"Of course, I'm sure. My friend wouldn't give me raw egg," Orion said,

"Are you going to eat it?" Ken-Yah asked.

"Yeah, I am."

"No, you're not." Sha-Nah tried to grab the egg from Orion, but Orion dodged her. One thing led to another, and the two girls were rolling around on the floor wrestling over a cracked egg.

"Y'all I'm so sorry; my friends are embarrassing," Ken-Yah said to the livestream.

Orion and Sha-Nah stopped wrestling and walked to the camera. Orion looked at Ken-Yah and laughed. "We apologize for whatever that was," Sha-Nah said to the livestream, laughed as well.

"We have to go now," Ken-Yah said to the fans. "Goodbye." She waved.

Sha-Nah and Orion waved as well to the camera. "Goodbye."

The live stream ended.

There was a brief moment of calm.

Suddenly, something exploded and the building shook.

The girls looked out of the window. They saw fire coming from below, as the building swayed.

Levi and Fletcher called them.

"Girls. Hotel Esoterica has been bombed," Levi said,

"The building's going to collapse; you need to get out of there immediately," Fletcher said.

Ken-Yah, Sha-Nah, and Orion stood at the window ledge as the building swayed.

"Midnight," Ken-Yah spoke to the AI in her key. "Three hover boards, now."

Three hover boards appeared in the air. The girls jumped out of the window onto the hover boards.

Three more bombs at different points of Hotel Esoterica went off, and the entire building collapsed.

Ken-Yah, Sha-Nah, and Orion were shocked.

However, before they could process what had happened, men in suits began to shoot at them.

"Midnight," Ken-Yah said, "motorcycles."

The hover boards changed into motorcycles with helmets. The Triptych Team landed on the road and swiftly drove away from the men in suits.

However, the men in suits soon caught up with the Triptych Team. They drove fast cars that had guns at the front. They shot rounds of bullets at the Triptych Team.

The Triptych Team dodged all the bullets.

"Midnight, gun," Ken-Yah said.

A gun materialized in her hand, and she shot one of the cars chasing them. She managed to destroy its engine and make it overturn.

They drove to a bridge just above Cyber Sea.

More of the suited men drove from the other side of the bridge.

The Triptych Team were trapped.

The suited men got out of their cars.

"Kill them," one of the men said.

The suited men attacked them.

Just then, Levi and Fletcher flew to the bridge in a spaceship. They jumped between the suited men and the Triptych Team.

Levi and Fletcher's swords were unbeatable, with the power to cut through anything, even cars.

Realizing that they were defeated, the suited men jumped off the bridge and into the water.

"Are you okay?" Levi asked the girls.

"We're okay," Sha-Nah replied.

Ken-Yah walked to the edge of the bridge and looked into the water. The suited men were gone.

"Where did they go?" Ken-Yah asked.

Sha-Nah, Orion, Levi, and Fletcher also walked to the edge of the bridge and looked at the water. It looked as though the suited men had jumped under the water and stayed there.

Race Five – Intergalactic

Ready. Set. Go!

The Triptych Team took the lead, blasting off right to the first position. Su-Ha and Jake came close to them at second position.

"Not today," Ken-Yah accelerated, taking on an unpredictable racing technique that involved slightly turning the back tires of the car to race in a sort of tilted position. This, paired with Sha-Nah's combustion flares gave the car an increased speed, causing the other racers not to catch up to them.

They crossed the finish line in no time as the winners of the race. The Triptych Team were the winners, followed by Su-Ha and Jake, Fletcher, and Levi, then Ni-ki and Ki-ra.

"The winners of this racing match are the Triptych Team," the announcer spoke.

The Triptych Team made their way to the high podium to receive their trophy.

"So, in your own words, what does the Triptych Team have to say about today's win?" A microphone floated in front of Ken-Yah.

She looked right into the camera. "You've all had a lot to say about us. Because we're an easy target for you. Well, the Sigma Trophy is an easy target for us to. And we'll show you all just who the hell we are. After this decade, you will learn to respect girls like me. We are not weak. We simply have a different way of doing things."

Meanwhile, the front man sat in his office, facing Cyber City, reading an augmented newspaper with the girls showcased as the winners of that race. He smirked. He turned around and face the clients who were present in his office. His clients looked impressed. They each had in front of them, screens that showcased the profiles of each of the girls. In real time, their online followings doubled and tripled.

He looked at a financial graph in front of him. It showed money flowing into his bank account and graphs rising. The money was coming in. All eyes were on the Triptych Team.

Race Six – Intergalactic

The sixth intergalactic race took place on two planets in the Sigma Galaxy. The Tómr planet—start. And the wolf planet—finish. A racetrack was built particularly for that race. The racers braced themselves as a machine counted down.

Ready. Set. Go!

The racers sped off. Fletcher and Levi took first place, the Triptych Team took second place, and Su-ha and Jake took third place.

Sha-Nah blasted a white flame into the combustion chamber and the car shot forward, leaving the other five racers far behind them.

The racetrack had numerous bumps on it; these scratched the bottom of the Tripych Team's car. Eventually it caused a hole to form at the bottom of the car.

Ken-Yah kept her focus on the road and on maneuvering the bumps as much as she could. Soon, they rose out of the surface of the Tómr planet and blasted forward.

Just ahead of them, a string of luminescent neon lights appeared. They continued going at full speed. The wolf planet appeared in full view ahead of them. A completely icy planet that with a rocky terrain.

Ken-Yah looked though the side mirror. She spotted Su-Ha and Jake closing in on them.

"Not today," she said. "Sha-Nah, go."

Sha-Nah leaped out of the car and into the air. With her fists, she formed large balls of fire that she shot at the Triptych Team's car, propelling it miles ahead. She flew back onto the roof of the car.

They finally entered the surface of the Wolf planet. It was beautiful. Everything was clear and icy. They drove at full speed across the rocky terrain.

Suddenly, Ken-Yah heard the howl of a wolf. Something about the wolf's howl caught her attention, and her eyes widened.

She looked to the side, where the wolf's howl had come from.

In the distance, she spotted a beautiful black wolf standing in front of a shining luminescent white tree.

The wolf looked at her with glistening purple eyes and howled one more time before it disappeared into thin air.

"Ken-Yah, focus!" Orion shouted.

Ken-Yah was knocked out of her thoughts. She looked ahead just in time to turn the car and avoid crashing into a rock. She looked into her mirror once again and spotted Su-Ha and Jake plus Fletcher and Levi closing in on them.

She pressed harder onto the accelerator and blasted forward. They crossed the finish line in no time, finishing in first place.

The girls sighed in relief.

"Another race won!" Orion shouted in glee. The girls hi-fived and fist bumped.

*

That night, in Hotel Esoterica, Ken-Yah, Sha-Nah, and Orion stood in the lobby as they waited for a visit from a guest. The girls wore formal suits, as their guest was a big investor.

Outside, fireworks glittered in celebration of the intergalactic quarter of the race finishing.

"Congratulations, girls," a voice of a man spoke.

The girls looked in the direction of the voice and saw a suited-up man enter the lobby with bodyguards following behind them, followed by the front man.

"Thank you, sir," the girls replied simultaneously.

"Girls, this is my client, Mr. Warrenheimer," the front man said.

"Hello, sir," Ken-Yah greeted.

"Hello there!" he replied.

He sat down; a screen full of numbers appeared in front of him. The numbers began to move up.

The three girls looked at each other. "We're listening," Ken-Yah said.

"That means you're bringing in lots of money and revenue to our planet," the front man said. "The entire Cosmos is tuning in to watch you."

"You probably don't recognize me; I don't go out much. I'm the heir to the CEO of the Maesun Company. And I'd like to sign you guys permanently," Mr. Warrenheimer said.

"You'll be funded and backed up, as you race under our company. I'm sure you've heard of our subsidiary—the knight laboratory, home to Cyber Planet XYZ's fleet of nights."

The girls' jaws dropped. "Of course, we've heard of the fleet of nights. The best swordsmen in the Sigma Galaxy," Sha-Nah said.

"We want to sponsor you; you'll be trained in racing further and backed financially." He pulled out a device and placed it on the table. He took a digital pen out of his pocket and placed it next to the device.

"In front of you is a contract. If you sign it, you've guaranteed yourself a life of success. We'll make you the best version of yourself beyond your wildest imagination." He spoke, "Fame, money, greatness, and power. It will all be yours if you sign this contract."

Ken-Yah looked at the contract in front of her. The words ran in her mind. Everything she ever wanted.

Fame, wealth, success…

She picked up the pen to sign the contract, but Sha-Nah held her hand.

"We have to think about it first," Sha-Nah said.

"I'll leave you to ponder on it and really think about it," Mr. Warrenheimer said, as he handed each of them a business card. "You can contact me whenever you're ready."

That night, Ken-Yah had insomnia; she could not sleep. She looked outside at the two moons of Cyber Planet XYZ.

We've qualified and passed all eight races. Two more races to go. We're up against the best and most experienced racers in the universe for the semi-finals and the finals. I don't care if I'm a rookie, I'll go after what I want.

That contract… Should I sign it? I need a definite lead.

Her mind wandered, and she began to think about the Wolf Planet.

She kept thinking about the shining white tree with luminescent branches and flowers. She remembered the dark wolf. How pretty it was, and how it looked straight at her.

She got out of her bed and dressed up. She wondered which jacket to wear. She picked the one she wore when she had first arrived in Cyber Planet XYZ.

She entered a spaceship that had been given to her by Mr. Warrenheimer on behalf of the Royal Maesun Company. As soon as she rose in the air, she left the surface of Cyber Planet XYZ. Passing the two moons, she headed for to the Wolf planet.

She drove across the icy terrain. The planet was freezing cold. Her way was lit by the pretty neon lights above. She spotted the shining tree once again and headed right to it.

Ken-Yah got out of the car and walked to the tree.

Snow began to fall.

On the trunk of the tree, neon silver letters began to appear.

Ken-Yah watched with utmost curiosity.

The letters formed a sentence on the tree trunk.

Take the blue pill.

She immediately thought of the blue pill that Vaughn had given her in the elevator on her first night in Cyber Planet XYZ. The blue pill that the Tuareg oracle had created for her.

She got a flashback of where she had kept the blue pill—the jacket.

She realized that she was wearing the same jacket that she had worn on that night.

Reaching into her pocket, she felt the glass case that had the blue pill. She brought it out of her pocket and opened it.

It began to glow. She looked at the writing on the tree once again.

Take the blue pill.

Without hesitation, she took the blue pill and swallowed it.

Ken-Yah's heart skipped a beat. She placed a hand on her chest that began to glow with a purple light.

Crystal blue lights ran from her heart to her veins. She was instantly transported to a space that resembled an infinitely large computer.

*

All around Ken-Yah were computer systems with numerous algorithms, wires, databases, and controls.

Ken-Yah walked around.

"Is anybody here?" she called out.

"Yes," a robotic voice said, startling Ken-Yah.

"Who are you?" she asked.

"I am infinite intelligence," the robotic voice replied. "You are in the super conscious."

"What is infinite intelligence?" Ken-Yah asked. "What is the super conscious? How did I get here? Did the blue pill get me here?"

"Infinite intelligence is the great universal intellect, the creative principle, the equation through which everything is formed," the robotic voice said.

Numbers and letters circled in equations around Ken-Yah.

"By choosing and taking the blue pill, you chose to be illuminated, to discover the truth of infinite intelligence," the robotic voice spoke. "Thus, you've chosen to discover the ultimate code to your destiny."

"In the super conscious, all thoughts and desires are deciphered," the voice asked. "I can hear your deepest thoughts and desires."

"You wish to be rich; you wish to be great. You wish to create a legacy for yourself," the robotic voice said. "But you should know the fundamental secret."

"I'm listening," Ken-Yah said.

"There is an infinite thinking substance through which all things are made. And which, in its original state, permeates, penetrates, and fills the interspaces of the universe," the voice said.

"The next time you need an ability or power, all you must do is take a statement and draw from the power of the infinite thinking substance."

"Why me?" Ken-Yah asked.

"Throughout the history of the Cosmos, ever since the big bang, I have worked with gifted people to catalyze the advancement of this universe. You are one of those people," the voice replied.

"I understand," Ken-Yah said. "I won't let you down."

Just then, a portal opened, and cheers were heard.

The coliseum appeared at the other end of the portal.

Ken-Yah walked into the portal.

As she walked, her clothes changed into her racing attire.

"Where Were You?" Orion asked.

"I took a breather," Ken-Yah replied.

The girls walked to the racecar and got in.

Ready. Set. Go!

The racers sped off. Su-ha and Jake took first place with the Triptych Team in second place. Fletcher and Levi in third place, Jung and Stallioná in fourth place, Ni-ki and Ki-ra in fifth place, and the Rhocancrians in sixth place. The racetrack reached out of Cyber Planet XYZ's surface, past the Sigma Star, and straight to Planet Inferno.

Upon entering the surface of Planet Inferno, the Triptych Team's car developed a protective layer to prevent the blasting lava below them from penetrating through the car. Planet Inferno was made of millions of active rumbling volcanos, each having eruptions in intervals of minutes.

The Triptych Team's car developed a set of turbo boosters and blasted forward.

Orion stood on top of the Triptych Team's RACE CAR with a serious look on her face.

"I'm not afraid of any lava," she spoke to herself. "I'm from Anhedonia, the planet's literally just made up of molten rock."

Her golden hair was tied in a ponytail as she held an electric guitar. She counted the intervals between the eruptions of the volcanoes and hit the strings just in time with an explosion of the lava. She played a loud death metal song on her electric guitar as Ken-Yah raced forward. It was pure craziness on her part; she wanted to stand outside and play a guitar because the possibility of getting hit by lava excited her.

Suddenly a large monster emerged from the furnace below; it was made from lava and rocks.

"Who dares interrupt my slumber?" the monster roared before hitting the racetrack. This caused the RACE CARS to fly in the air briefly before settling on the racetrack once again.

The monster raised its large rocky arm and descended onto the racetrack.

Orion rolled her eyes. "Ain't nobody coming to see you, Otis?"

She pressed a button on her guitar, and it turned into a gun. She pointed it toward the monster and shot, hitting it right on the forehead, causing it to stumble backward and fall back into the lava.

Orion looked ahead and spotted the finishing line. However, there seemed to be a gap in the road.

Orion then jumped out of the car and dived into the lava.

She blasted out of the lava to view the gap in the track. The road seemed to be breaking. Her eyes widened at how large the gap was. Below it, there was a red-hot whirlpool of churning molten rock.

Orion dived back into the lava and swam back to where the Triptych Team's car was. She propelled herself upward onto the racetrack and jumped back into the Triptych Team's car.

"The gap is too big," Orion said, "you won't be able to make it. I can swim through the lava. But you guys, you'll surely perish if you fall in."

"What should we do then?" Sha-Nah asked. The car was still going at full speed.

Fletcher and Levi had already stopped their car. Levi looked at the Triptych Team's car going at full speed. He had a surprised expression on his face.

"Ken-Yah!" Orion yelled. "You need to stop and turn back now. Levi and Fletcher have done exactly that. All the other teams have."

"Get in," Ken-Yah said, "we're making the leap. Get in and hold on tight."

Orion got in. Sha-Nah closed her eyes and braced herself. The car sped forward and got closer to the gap in the road. Ken-Yah drove forward at maximum speed.

The car sparked, and her eyes began to glow a clear white color.

She drove past the gap, leaping over the lava,

"In life, you just gotta Leap Forward," Ken-Yah said as the car flew above the lava.

They landed on the other end of the racetrack.

The speed at which they were going doubled.

They got closer to the finish line.

"Woohoo!" Orion yelled. "Speed! Spunk! Stamina!"

They crossed the finish line and won the race.

Chapter Six

The next day, Ken-Yah sat in the Triptych Team's car in the garage. Her back faced the door which was slightly open.

Someone entered the garage through the door, dressed in combat gear and holding a gun.

He pointed it at Ken-Yah and shot.

To his dismay, sand flooded the floor, flowing out of the lifelike dummy doll that Ken-Yah had created to look like her.

He then realized it was a trap.

However, the real Ken-Yah was on the ceiling, in her Star-Hero costume. He did not see her.

She silently got down from the ceiling and stood behind him.

She tapped his shoulder. He turned around, and she punched him. The Star-Hero Suit had the ability of a 'super punch' that knocked opponents out cold.

The man fell to the ground.

Ken-Yah checked his pockets and pulled out an identification card. It had nothing except for a QR code.

"AI, activate super smell," Ken-Yah said to the AI in the Star Hero suit.

Ken-Yah took a whiff of the identification card. She immediately caught the origin of the card using scent recognition.

It was coming from the Cyber City Sewers.

"I'm gonna find out who's trying to sabotage the tournament. And I'm gonna stop that person," she said to herself.

She followed the scent. It led her away from Cyber City to Cyber Sea.

Under the bridge of Cyber Sea, there was a large tunnel into the sewers of the city. She stood at the entrance of the tunnel. A grumbling sound emitted from deep within the sewers.

The mask of the Star-Hero Suit had a see-through ability. Ken-Yah activated the ability and saw far into the tunnel. There was a web of tunnels, all leading to one central operation point that was highly guarded. It was a lab of some sort.

Ken-Yah activated the invisible ability of the Star-Hero Suit. She jumped across the walls of the tunnel and made her way to a tunnel that led downward. She jumped into it and silently landed in a laboratory full of scientists in lab coats and gas masks. They had lifeforms in tubes. Lifeforms that Ken-Yah had never seen before.

Some lifeforms were amphibian and some were reptilian. However, they were not completely evolved lifeforms.

The scientists studied them and shipped them to different areas of the facility.

Suddenly, one scientist made eye contact with another.

He walked to a certain spot in the laboratory.

The other scientist threw something to him. He held his hand out to catch it. However, midair, it released a wave of sulfuric acid. The sulfuric acid caused Ken-Yah to faint, and the invisible ability on the Star-Hero Suit was turned off.

The scientists stood around Ken-Yah. She was taken and locked up.

Ken-Yah woke up in a chamber deeper in the ground, tied up to a chair.

She was back in her normal clothes, but the Star-Hero ring was still on her finger. She could not see anything because she was blindfolded. She was too weak to move any limb in her body. The scientists had drugged her, making her incapable of any movement.

She sat in silence in the chamber. Faintly, she could hear growling coming from somewhere. Something sinister was going on down there. She was afraid. She couldn't move, and she was locked up in an underground chamber in a facility with strange lifeforms and shady scientists.

*

Meanwhile on Earth 2, Jarvien took a nap in his Vaporwave City luxury apartment. The beautiful red sunset lightly peered into his room as he slept peacefully.

His peaceful sleep was interrupted when glimpses of Ken-Yah tied up in a chamber flooded his consciousness. His body cells began to vibrate and shift. His body became blurry.

Suddenly, he found himself in the underground room that Ken-Yah was locked in.

"Ken-Yah?"

She remained unresponsive.

"That's right, she probably can't hear me," he said to himself.

He looked at his hands. They were blurry and glitching.

"I must've lost control of my powers once again."

He heard grumbling coming from outside of the room. He walked through the wall and saw the grizzliest thing he could ever imagine.

Lifeforms, some botched, some strange as hell, locked in capsules, as scientists shipped them around.

An uneasy feeling took over his body, telling him to look to his right. He looked and saw a portal. Out of the portal came humanoid creatures that looked like they had come straight from hell.

"Demogorgons," Jarvien whispered in disbelief. "They're supposed to be locked away in The Realm of Giants. Someone's opened up a portal. What the hell is going on here?"

Jarvien… Jarvien…

He had a distant voice calling him—Santino's voice. The voice became louder and louder until Jarvien woke up in his bed with a gasp of air. Santino sat by his side.

"Jarvien, are you okay?" Santino asked as he handed Jarvien a glass of water. Jarvien took the water.

"Did you lose control of your powers again?" he asked.

"Yes," Jarvien replied.

"What did you see?" Santino asked.

"Ken-Yah's in trouble," Jarvien said. "She's locked in a facility under Cyber City. Something shady's going on."

*

Jarvien and Santino walked through Cyber City as the sun was setting.

Santino held a gadget that he had designed to track unusual thermal activities. As they walked, they reached a house in one of the suburbs.

Jarvien closed his eyes, feeling the energy of the house and using it to fuel his vision.

Suddenly, he travelled to a different time but the same building. His physical body was still with Santino, but his consciousness was split between two different moments in time, the past and the present.

In the vision of the past, Jarvien looked into the house and saw his classmate and friend Fulcrum, whom he had last seen four years ago, in high school.

Fulcrum looked to be having an argument with someone. An older man, who appeared to be Fulcrum's father, was yelling at him and slapping him continuously for failing the school semester.

"You're a disgrace," his father said. "You'll never amount to anything."

His father slapped him and spat in his face. Fulcrum remained still; he didn't move.

"I send you to the best school on Earth and this is what you fucking bring me?" his dad yelled. "The school says they're gonna hold you back; you're not going to graduate with the rest of your classmates."

"It was a rough school year," Fulcrum said. "I was really depressed and—"

"Depression, my ass," his dad interrupted. "Do you think I'm stupid? There's lots of people with depression who always get shit done. Depression isn't an excuse for you to flunk in school."

"And what the fuck is this?" His dad faced his phone screen to Fulcrum. "Is this what I sacrifice my money for? Instead of studying, you've been out there wasting time with some dumbasses?"

The screen showed a viral video on the internet of Fulcrum skating with Santino, Jarvien, Dionysus, and a girl called Erica after school. They were laughing and having lots of fun. It was on Dionysus' online stream and had trillions of views from across the Cosmos. The video also showed him kissing Erica—his girlfriend.

"You think you're hot shit just because you're friends with these sissy boys who dance on the internet and play video games all day?"

His father slapped him once again. He was burning with anger.

"Get the fuck out of my house," his dad snapped. "You're on your own now. Don't call me your dad, and don't ever reach out to me. Pack your shit and get out."

Fulcrum walked through Cyber City with his suitcases. He had nowhere to go. His plan was to find somewhere to sleep and then leave for Earth the next day through the space metro station.

He booked a hotel room for the night. He showered and rested on the bed. His wet hair was curly as water dripped down his chest.

He felt low. His depression came over him like a dark cloud.

Fulcrum turned on his phone and texted Erica. It was only her that could get him in a brighter mood.

She didn't reply immediately, so he just scrolled through his gallery, looking at pictures of them together… kissing, cuddling, just doing cute stuff that couples do.

He tried to call his best friend Dionysus, who he always confided in. Dionysus wasn't answering.

After around thirty minutes of Erica not answering, Fulcrum called her.

She answered. "Hey! Fulcrum! How are you? I'm so glad you called; I've been meaning to talk to you about something."

"Sure, you okay?" Fulcrum asked.

He genuinely cared about her; she was his everything.

"I'm okay!" Erica replied.

Little did Fulcrum know that as Erica was talking to him, she was in bed with his friend, Dionysus—who was kissing her neck.

"I need a break," she spoke, "from the relationship!"

Fulcrum paused. "Huh?"

"I need a breakup," she said, out of breath as Dionysus kissed her neck. "As in, I don't want to be in a relationship with you anymore. It's been fun but like, your depression has been taking a toll on me, and I wanna be with someone a bit happier."

That hurt Fulcrum. "But I can work on it," he said. "You can just talk to me and tell me what you need; we can work on it together."

"I can't! I'm sorry," Erica said and she hung up the call.

Fulcrum was shocked. He looked at the sunset outside. So much had happened to him that evening.

He decided to go for a walk to clear his head.

He walked to the Cyber Bridge and sat on the edge, looking at the Cyber Sea below. There were rocks right below him.

Suddenly, he felt his phone buzz. He checked it, hoping it was a text from Erica. But it wasn't. It was a notification from an online news page.

His eyes widened as he read it.

Breaking news: Internet celebrity—Dionysus—seen with new girl on romantic date in Vaporwave City.

It showed a picture of Erica and Dionysus holding hands, walking into a restaurant and kissing.

Fulcrum couldn't believe his eyes. It all added up. His girl had cheated on him with his best friend and now they were dating.

He sighed. A tear dropped down from his eyes and fell down to the rocks below.

He stayed silent for a moment, listening to the waves of the sea. He breathed in and out. He had been through so much. He was tired.

"If I jumped headfirst, the impact on those rocks would kill me," he spoke to himself.

"Death would be nice," he said to himself. "It would be a nice break from all of this."

There was a moment of silence. More tears fell from his eyes as a slight breeze blew past him. With non-resistance, he let his body lean over, and he fell from the bridge.

He fell and landed on the rocks below.

He landed with a harsh blow. His body lay in a pool of blood.

After some time, the waves of the sea that splashed against the rocks carried his body away. He drifted in the water, sinking deep until he reached the bottom.

Fulcrum was dead—that is, until a glowing life form swam to his body and attached itself to his spine.

He opened his eyes. They were glowing. The life form has brought him back to life.

He then looked behind him and swam to the underwater cave that the life form had come from. It led to a larger cave just below the land surface, where he was able to breathe air. And in that cave, there were numerous other life forms. Trapped in the darkness below Cyber City.

He had read about these lifeforms. Many of them had occupied Cyber City before the human race of Cyber Planet XYZ colonized the planet. However, everybody thought that the original lifeforms of the planet had gone extinct. It turns out they hadn't, they had just been pushed underground.

Fulcrum frowned as he remembered the cruel things that had been done to him by his fellow humans.

"I will put an end to all of them," he said to himself.

Fulcrum immediately got to work. And within four years, he had built an operational base under Cyber City, with the most lethal weapons and tunnels running across the planet.

"I will create an army of creatures and unleash them onto the city. If that fails, I will sink the entire city and burn the whole planet," he said to himself.

*

That was the end of Jarvien's vision. He returned back to the present, where he and Santino stood in Cyber City. He looked at Santino.

"What did you see?" Santino asked.

"It's Fulcrum," Jarvien said.

"From high school?" Santino asked.

"Yes. He's turned into a villain; he has a large base under Cyber City. He's built an army, and he's planning an attack on the entire planet," Jarvien said. "If the attack fails, he plans to sink the entire planet and kill everybody."

Santino turned on his machine. It showed him all the tunnels that had been created under Cyber City. He spotted one area that was high in thermal radiation.

"That must be Fulcrum's layer," Santino said.

*

Ken-Yah struggled to free herself from the chair when she regained control of her body. The chair fell over instead. She was still blindfolded, so she couldn't see.

Just then, the door opened.

A handsome, good-looking, tall young man walked in with two bodyguards behind him.

His hair was long and wavy. A handsome young man with a playful but devious smile. He got off the platform and walked to Ken-Yah.

His bodyguards adjusted Ken-Yah's chair and took off her blindfold.

He sat on a chair in front of Ken-Yah with his legs wide open, facing her. They made eye contact.

He smirked.

*

"Well, if it isn't the leader of the Triptych Team," the handsome young man said to Ken-Yah. "Pardon my manners, I didn't introduce myself. I'm Fulcrum," he spoke.

"What the hell is going on here?" Ken-Yah asked. "Why have you been trying to kill me?"

"Because I bet on Su-Ha and Jake to fund my project. But your abrupt entrance into the race made me lose money. I wasn't trying to kill you. I was trying to abduct you and keep you out of the races till the final. But I see you've come to me yourself," Fulcrum replied. "But no worries now, I was able to complete my project without the extra funding."

"What project?" Ken-Yah asked.

"I'm glad you asked," Fulcrum replied.

A reel began to play in front of Ken-Yah.

"The first inhabitants of Cyber Planet XYZ were reptillianoid animals. They lived in peace. Until the Cyberians arrived and wiped them all out of existence," he spoke.

"I've been working on a plan to bring the original reptilianoids back to Cyber Planet XYZ and restore its natural form," Fulcrum said.

"For years, everyone on Cyber Planet XYZ thought that the reptilianoid animals had gone extinct. That is until my scientists found remains of their genetics in the Cyber Sea."

"I launched a project to bring the reptilianoids back to existence. We succeeded, and for two years now, I've been growing an army of reptilianoids under Cyber City. I'll wipe out all humans from this planet, and then I'll expand my plan to Earth."

"You're planning to wipe out Cyber Planet XYZ?" Ken-Yah asked.

"Exactly," Fulcrum replied. "Cyberians are humans that came from Earth a long time ago and mixed with other humanoid species in the Sigma Galaxy. But Cyber Planet XYZ was never theirs. They carried out a massacre of the reptilianoid creatures, just like they did with the dinosaurs on Earth when they landed there from Sirius B. Earth was never theirs, and neither was Cyber Planet XYZ."

"Why do you care so much about this?" Ken-Yah asked.

Fulcrum pulled out a knife and cut through an area on his arm.

It turned into hard reptilianoid skin and regenerated immediately.

"I've got some reptilianoid genes in my blood. I was saved from death by one of those lifeforms. All my life, I felt like an outsider. But not anymore. I learnt the truth about humans. Do you wish to know the truth, Ken-Yah? Can your pretty little mind handle the truth?"

Fulcrum was electric, enticing. His energy filled the room. He had a huge star power and sexual energy to him.

"Would you consider joining my team? Doing bad shit with me? I know you've got a firecracker in you," he spoke.

"I would never destroy mankind," Ken-Yah said. "I'm not evil."

"I guess you've got a lot of growing up to do then," Fulcrum said as he got up.

"Everybody has a villain in them," he said, "it's just gotta come out at the right time."

He adjusted his jacket, wore his shades, and walked out of the room.

A television in the corner of the room turned on and began to play a stream of Cyber City from an aerial view. The song 'Fly Me to the Moon' played in the background.

The door closed shut. Ken-Yah was left wondering how she would escape.

Fulcrum walked powerfully to a large military shuttle that waited for him. A line of bodyguards stood on either side of the entrance.

Fulcrum walked into the military shuttle and sat in the pilot chamber.

Legions of Demogorgons marched into the cargo area of the military ship as well as a fleet of soldiers in Fulcrum's army.

"Where are we going, Master?" one of Fulcrum's pilots asked.

Fulcrum looked forward. He had a sure and determined look on his face as a large wormhole opened in front of the military shuttle.

"You'll see," he spoke. "Just fly ahead."

The military shuttle flew into the wormhole and it closed.

*

Meanwhile, the scientists began to release the reptilianoids onto Cyber Planet XYZ. They took the cages to the tunnels and opened them. The bloodthirsty reptilianoids ran to Cyber City and climbed out of the sewers.

Soon, they had filled the city. They climbed up buildings, destroyed cars, and attacked anyone in sight.

Ken-Yah watched it all happen from the television in the chamber she was locked in.

She tried to press the ring on her finger and change into her Star-Hero Suit. But there was a problem with it. The sulfuric acid from earlier must have tampered with it. She remembered the AI system within the Star-Hero Suit.

"Midnight, activate Star-Hero Suit," she spoke.

"Star-Hero Suit activated," a robot voice replied.

Ken-Yah immediately jumped out of the chair in her Star-Hero Suit.

She kicked the door, trying to break it down. She punched it, pushed it, and everything she could do.

*

Meanwhile, Jarvien and Santino had just landed in Fulcrum's lair and walked through an empty laboratory. All the scientists had packed up and disappeared.

Santino's machine detected the chamber that Ken-Yah was being held in, and they made their way to it.

They stood at the door, and it appeared that someone inside was kicking it.

Jarvien placed his hand on the handle and simply opened it.

"Ken-Yah?" Jarvien said, unsure if it was her because she was in the Star-Hero Suit.

"Jarvien! Santino!" she spoke.

"Sis, it was literally open," Jarvien said referring to the door.

Ken-Yah walked outside and hugged Jarvien and Santino.

"Some evil guy called Fulcrum is planning to destroy Cyber City," she spoke.

"We know, sis," Jarvien said, "he's been planning."

"But right now, he's gone." Santino added. "We tried to track him, but it appears that he has disappeared with all his scientists. The attack on Cyber Planet XYZ risks wiping out the entire planet and the entire Sigma Galaxy."

"Well, I'll stop them," Ken-Yah said as she ran to a tunnel that led upward.

"Ken-Yah, how are you going to stop an army of those creatures alone?" Jarvien asked.

"I can do it," Ken-Yah said. "I can do anything."

She flew upward, swiftly making her way to the entrance of the layer.

She flew out of the layer, only to find Cyber City up in flames.

The reptilianoid animals were running rampant and destroying everything.

Ken-Yah ran across the buildings in the Star Hero costume. She saved people from falling buildings and fought the reptilianoid monsters who were trying to eat civilians.

Her attention was taken by the cry of a child in the distance. She spotted twins who were standing together amidst all the chaos. A building was about to fall on them.

She flew to them and got them out of the way. The building collapsed, but she flew the twins to safety.

As Ken-Yah ran across the buildings, she felt a jolt of electricity running through her body.

"If I could channel electric current through the Star Hero suit, I could find a way to annihilate all these reptilianoid animals," she said.

She did exactly that. She jumped onto an electricity pole and tore the wire. She placed the wire on her wrist, and the Star Hero Suit absorbed the electricity.

She then flew above Cyber City to a vantage point.

The Star-Hero Suit sparked with electricity. Then, she zoomed in on the reptilianoid animals. One by one, she blasted them with an electric current.

"Fuck it, I'm gonna help her," Jarvien said.

He transformed into "The Quantum Leaper"—a combat suit that Santino made for him.

It was made of Uranium and enabled him to split the atomic particles of his body between different dimensions and different points in time without getting him worn out.

The suit had uranium wings which sprouted majestically into the air.

"Be safe," Santino said.

Jarvien flew out of the sewers up into the sky above Cyber City.

Hovering in the air, he watched the reptilianoid monsters destroy everything. Civilians ran for their lives as the entire place was burning in flames.

He flew down, carrying as many civilians as he could to safety and fighting the monsters with the super strength of the Quantum Leaper Suit.

He spotted Ken-Yah in the distance, blasting the reptilianoid monsters with electricity from her Star-Hero Suit. He flew toward her.

However, Star-Hero did not see the largest reptilianoid which climbed up a building and jumped at her. It grabbed her and smashed her into a building.

She tried to hit the reptilianoid, but it was too strong.

She landed on an office table. She got up and looked at the reptilianoid. It walked on four legs, and its face was heavily disfigured. It charged toward her.

Ken-Yah adjusted her Star-Hero Suit.

"I've got a race to win." She pointed her hands at the reptilianoid. "So, if you don't mind, kindly get out of my way."

Electricity blasters formed on her hands.

She blasted the reptilianoid with a lightning bolt. It was unphased and unmoved; it continued to run toward her.

Ken-Yah increased the level of lightning that she blasted toward it.

Lighting emitted from her eyes as she screamed with rage. Why won't you just die?

There was an explosion, and the monster fell out of the building to its death.

Ken-Yah climbed out of the building and hung out of the window. All the reptilianoids were gone. The Intergalactic Military had gotten rid of them.

However, the entire city was up in flames.

Ken-Yah hovered above the burning Cyber City.

People took videos as she hung from the window. They could not tell who it was because of the mask. They could only see the word 'Star-Hero.' They began to cheer for her, "Star Hero! Star Hero! Star Hero!"

"People of Cyber City!" She shouted. "The show must go on."

The citizens cheered for her.

"To the coliseum." She flew to the Cyber City Coliseum.

She entered the coliseum changing room and quickly changed into her final and advanced Sigma Space Racing Suit—the Final Boss.

Then she ran to Sha-Nah and Orion who had been waiting for her.

"Where were you?" Sha-Nah asked.

"Fighting some bad guys," Ken-Yah replied.

"Wait," Orion said, "was this you?"

She showed Ken-Yah an online video captioned 'Star Hero saves the day.'

"Yeah," Ken-Yah said.

Ken-Yah chuckled. "Let's do this thing," she said.

Final Race

The countdown began. Ken-Yah looked directly ahead as she held the steering wheel tightly. The engines rumbled. Ready! Set! Go!

The car sped off into the distance on the neon lit racetrack that led up into the sky and outside of the planet. The vehicles raced in high speed. The purple galaxy around them glittered as the girls felt the adrenaline running through their veins.

Ken-Yah nodded at Sha-Nah, who released a fiery ball of a red flame into the combustion chamber, blasting the car forward at full speed. The racetrack twirled around Cyber Planet XYZ's purple rings and went around two other planets in the Sigma Galaxy.

In the distance, numerous colored constellations glittered. There was a cloud of glittery purple space dust that crossed the racetrack. The girls watched in awe, before getting back to the race.

As they drove, one of their tires burst, causing them to fall off track. The car overturned as it steered off.

Sha-Nah climbed out of the car to fix the tire as they spiraled off the track.

"Kaizen healing ability, activate."

A ball of matter formed in her hands that she directed to the tire, which got fixed immediately via atomic fusion.

She climbed back inside the car. They got back onto the track and continued the race.

They went at full speed, taking first position and leaving every team behind.

Suddenly, a collection of laser bullets began to fire toward their direction.

"What the hell!" Ken-Yah exclaimed.

The girls looked behind. There was a large spaceship behind them. It fired laser bullets continuously at them.

A fleet of Fulcrum's soldiers were attacking them.

"The ammunition on that spaceship looks deadly," Sha-Nah said. Ken-Yah maneuvered through the laser bullets that swarmed their way.

A fleet of smaller battle ships emerged from the large spaceship and flew to them. Fulcrum's guards shot at them.

Ken-Yah dodged them with her fluid navigation skills.

Orion leaped out of the car and headed straight at the battleships.

"Orion!" Ken-Yah and Sha-Nah called out, concerned.

Orion ran across the battle ships with two laser katana swords in her hand. She cut across their engines and firearm points, causing them to malfunction and stop.

A group of Fulcrum's men emerged from the spaceship to fight Orion.

She smirked as they approached her, holding her swords tightly. They lunged at her; she dodged their hits as she struck at them with her swords, jumping from battleship to battleship as she fought off each of them, trying to get to the main battleship.

The pilot on the largest battleship pressed a red button and more fighters emerged.

Orion did her best to fight them all off. But she got overpowered and ran back to the RACE CAR.

"Go help her," Ken-Yah said to Sha-Nah. "I'll find a way to win the race."

Sha-Nah nodded and leaped out of the RACE CAR; she lunged up into the air onto the battleships.

She used her combat Kaizen martial arts skills as Orion used her special sword technique. They fought off Fulcrum's guards who attacked from left to right. They were able to destroy all the battleships. However, the main one still hurled laser bullets at the Triptych Team's car.

Meanwhile, on the racetrack, Ken-Yah accelerated as much as she could to reach the other racers. Sha-Nah and

Orion leaped onto the RACE CAR and began to individually block the bullets.

Suddenly, another spaceship appeared right in front of them. A more lethal looking battleship.

There were two gigantic canons at the front of the ship, with nuclear radiation within them.

"There's more of them," Orion said.

"They're planning to blast us with nuclear radiation," Sha-Nah said.

Ken-Yah looked helplessly from inside the car.

"If we get blasted…" she mouthed to herself, "we'll surely die."

The canons loaded. Ken-Yah closed her eyes as the canons blasted toward them.

But nothing happened. Instead, from the corner of her eye, she could see a shining light. She looked up.

Sha-Nah had stopped the radioactive blast with her own radioactive wave that she had formed.

Orion watched in awe.

Sha-Nah had formed a massive shield of radioactive energy that blocked the blasts of the canon.

With both hands, she sustained the shield.

The force of the impact shook the entire racetrack and formed an explosion seen everywhere in the universe, even as far as the Milky Way Galaxy.

Sha-Nah moved one hand to point at the spaceship on her left. The beastly man blasted another radioactive wave. But that radioactive wave collided with Sha-Nah's own radioactive wave. She blocked both attacks from the left and right.

The force of the radioactive energy was overwhelming. It eventually began to flow through her. Her entire body began to glow silver.

"Ken-Yah, Orion. Go!" she shouted. "I'll be fine!"

Ken-Yah sped off as Orion got back into the car.

Ken-Yah exerted as much force as she could, accelerating the car to its limit.

Her hand held the staring wheel tightly, to the point that her knuckles were pale, and her veins were popping out.

Suddenly, a shock wave blasted from the car, and Ken-Yah's body developed a layer of lightning. The shock sent the car miles ahead on the racetrack.

The commentator yelled into the microphone, "Oh my gosh! The Triptych Team's car is completely covered in lightning."

The crowd roared in excitement.

Orion looked at Ken-Yah. "You're emitting lightning."

Ken-Yah laughed. "Yeah, baby, I am. And it feels exhilarating." The car went faster, approaching the racers in third place.

The entire car began to shoot lightning off the racetrack, producing as much electricity as it could. The car let out loud cracking sounds, like a firecracker.

"I don't know what's happening, but it's making the car go faster," Ken-Yah said as she turned the wheel.

The Triptych Team's car went faster and faster on the racetrack.

The car released another shockwave and went faster, taking first place.

Sha-Nah blasted Fulcrum's battleships with one large radioactive wave, stunning their ammunition. She then jumped back to the racetrack.

Suddenly, Levi and Fletcher flew onto the racetrack from two portals. They fought Fulcrum's soldiers.

Sha-Nah flew closer to the car as it reached first place, jumping onto it just seconds away from the finish line.

The three girls braced themselves as they crossed the finish line, leaving a trail of fire behind them.

For a moment, it felt as though the world had stopped. Every spectator in the universe paused.

The impossible had been done. The unexpected happened. The four winds of success had blown to them their rightful victory… as has always and will always happen to girls of their nature.

"Ladies and Gentlemen, this year's Sigma Space Race Champions, the Triptych Team!" the announcer shouted.

Everyone that watched cheered for them. Even people that did not support them clapped in approval.

The front man and his clients clapped as they watched from a V.I.P. area in the Coliseum. They were impressed.

Everyone in Cyber City cheered for the Triptych Team as billboards showed pictures of them. Fireworks were blown into the air as everybody cheered.

Jarvien, filled with love, happiness, and excitement, hugged Santino.

"They won! They won!" Jarvien said in absolute happiness as he looked at the screen above.

Evora, the news reporter from the Andromeda Galaxy, even started crying because she had watched the entire tournament rooting for the girls—after all, they reminded her so much of herself. And if they could achieve something that big, then that meant that she too could achieve everything that her heart desired. She wiped her tears of joy and clapped as she looked at the screen.

The Triptych Team stood for pictures as cameras flew all around them, getting a 360 view of the young firecrackers.

The school racing coach watched from The Earthian Milky Way School—the racing coach that told Ken-Yah she would never amount to anything. His face was filled with dread, for he realized what he had done was a huge mistake. He looked at the floor as a great wave of shame took over him. His judgement day had reached… as it always does, for people of his nature.

Ken-Yah let out a sigh of relief.

"Thank you God, thank you so much, I'll never doubt you one bit," she said quietly.

Vaughn walked onto the racetrack from a portal. He scanned the area as he looked for Ken-Yah.

He finally spotted her; she saw him too.

She ran to him and jumped into his arms.

"Are you all right?" he asked.

"I'm okay," Ken-Yah replied.

Just then, a portal opened in front of them that led back to the Cyber Planet XYZ Coliseum. They walked into the portal.

Cameras surrounded them as pictures were taken. Lights flashed all around them as the crowd cheered. Fireworks shot up in the air as the crowd chanted their names.

Amidst the excitement, a glowing pentagram formed below Ken-Yah, Sha-Nah, and Orion.

The ground on which the girls stood turned into a platform that rose into the air.

Neon colors surrounded them as their outfits were transformed into neon purple racing suits, and they were each handed trophies of recognition.

The platform continued to rise, until a fancy golden spaceship materialized above them.

"This spaceship is from Solaris," Ken-Yah said.

The door of the golden spaceship opened.

They were surprised at who they saw when they entered. The D.V.F. The most famous group of warriors in the Cosmos.

A woman approached them. She was dressed in elegant wear and looked fancy. She had the prettiest caramel skin and purple hair that the girls had ever seen.

"Hello, girls, congratulations on your win. My name is Miss Hubur, Leader of the D.V.F.," she spoke.

"Hello, Ken-Yah." She smiled fondly at her.

"Hi." Ken-Yah smiled back, feeling happy to see her.

Ken-Yah had met Hubur on a few occasions. To others, Hubur was the leader of the D.V.F. But to Ken-Yah, she was Jarvien's loving mom.

They followed Miss Hubur to an elevator and were transported upward.

As the elevator traveled, there was a shaky feeling.

However, the elevator kept on going. The door opened to a high-tech room.

The room had glass walls and stared out to a neon-esque aesthetic of Cyber City.

"It looks like we're in Hotel Esoterica," Ken-Yah said.

"No, we're in Hotel Dionysia," Miss Hubur said.

She pressed a button on the table. The ceiling opened.

Above them was another, equally identical, Cyber City. Only, it was upside down.

The girls looked up. The buildings were the same, glittered the same, and everything was the same.

"Cyber Planet XYZ exists as a dual dimension," Miss Hubur said. "That is what it has in common with Earth. Very few people know this though."

"On the racetrack, do you realize what you did?" Miss Hubur turned around and asked Ken-Yah.

"What did I do?" Ken-Yah asked.

"You broke into interdimensional speed with the amount of quantum energy you exuded," Miss Hubur said.

"The sheer force of breaking the interdimensional barrier caused a few electrons within you to alter, hence, you acquired lightning firecracker powers—the ability to use heat and light energy to increase the speed at which you are going at any moment. In other words, Ken-Yah, your molecules altered, and now you have the power of super speed."

The room morphed and turned into a field.

"Test it," Miss Hubur said. "Run."

Ken-Yah braced herself. She ran across the field and back in exactly one second.

"Woah," she said.

The field then morphed back into the room.

Miss Hubur continued to speak.

"We want to recruit you for our Quantum Research Program. We believe that studying your ability will give us insight on how to enter pockets of existence that exist between dimensions."

"Sure, no problem," Ken-Yah said.

She trusted Hubur because Hubur was just like a mother to her. Orion and Sha-Nah were skeptical though.

"Don't worry," Ken-Yah said. "She's my friend's mom."

Orion and Sha-Nah eased up.

"We'll need you to sign up for an oath of protection," Hubur said. "You're now sort of celebrities in a way, and many eyes are on you."

There was a fingerprint area. The girls each placed their fingerprints onto the area.

Ken-Yah looked at Miss Hubur. "Thank you," she said.

"You're welcome, my darling," Miss Hubur replied.

Ken-Yah smiled at her, purple eyes glistening as well.

"You should get back to Cyber City. The press is probably wondering where you are," Miss Hubur said.

Miss Hubur opened a portal to Cyber City, and the girls walked in.

The city was flooded with paparazzi and reporters. Some reporting on the Triptych Team's awesome win, some reporting on the mysterious 'Star Hero,' who has saved Cyber City from the reptilianoid monsters. So much was going on.

Thanks to the high technology of Cyber Planet XYZ, the city was fixed and back to its usual glamor. There were parties going on everywhere.

Evora from the Andromeda Galaxy teen news ran to the Triptych Team. "Girls, how do you feel after your win?"

"We feel good," Orion said into the microphone.

There fans from all over the Cosmos made edits and fan-cams of them.

That night, there was a party in one of Cyber City's hotels. Ken-Yah, Sha-Nah, and Orion attended. Vaughn attended as well. Levi and Fletcher attended as well. Jarvien and Santino were there too.

Vaughn and Ken-Yah danced together.

Su-Ha and Jake tried to enter, but security didn't let them in. They watched from outside as the Triptych Team danced and had fun.

Final Chapter

The Sigma Space Racing Tournament was over. The girls each received fifty million Earthian dollars in their bank accounts.

They also each received permanent travel passes and residential permits to any planet in the Cosmos.

Pictures of them filled every news stream in the universe, as the girls that had made history and broken the status quo—proving that teenage girls had just as much power as any other racer in the universe.

Orion read an augmented newspaper in their hotel room as they packed their bags. The front page showed her, Sha-Nah, and Ken-Yah.

The newspaper told the story of their chaotic rise to the championship and showed their interview after they received the grand prize.

Ken-Yah and Sha-Nah joined Orion next to her chair and read the article with her.

Sha-Nah received a text on her phone. "Your ride is here."

"The ride is here," Sha-Nah said.

"Oh, sweet," Orion said and got up.

The girls walked outside and found a Limousine waiting for them.

*

They were driven to a large high-tech building. Two Olympian statues stood at the entrance. The building was labeled: The Royal Maesun Company.

They entered the building and walked to the reception.

"We're here to see Mr. Warrenheimer," Ken-Yah spoke.

"Yes, of course," the receptionist said. "Please have a seat in the waiting area labeled Sigma Space Races as I contact him."

"Sure."

Ken-Yah, Sha-Nah, and Orion walked to the waiting lobby. The waiting areas were divided into various categories. They looked for the one labeled Sigma Space Races and entered it.

The winners of various Sigma Space Races were showcased on the walls. In glass cases, the various trophies over the years were displayed.

Ken-Yah noticed crumpled paper in a tiny glass case. She opened it and read it.

I hypothesize the existence of more than one dimension on Earth, through which mass and energy can move from. The ability of certain properties to move between these dimensions is rooted in kinetic power. I also hypothesize that it is through constant interchangeability between both dimensions, at a high level of kinesis, that the altering of physical attributes is possible. There is also a possibility of pockets of existence between two dimensions.

Swiss Federal Polytechnic School – Earth 1.

Final year student – Albert Einstein

"Mr. Warrenheimer is ready to see you now," the receptionist said to the Triptych Team.

They entered an elevator that led them to Mr. Warrenheimer's office. They walked in.

He sat in his chair, facing Cyber City outside.

When they entered the room, he turned around and welcomed them.

"Welcome," he said. "I have something to show you. Please, follow me."

Ken-Yah, Sha-Nah, and Orion followed him. They entered an elevator.

The elevator led to a large facility.

There were advanced racing cars of all kinds. The girls looked at the cars in awe.

"This is a racer's heaven," Sha-Nah said.

"Welcome to the life of a Space Racing Champion," Mr. Warrenheimer said to them.

The Triptych Team looked on in awe. Their hearts beat with excitement.

www.ingramcontent.com/pod-product-compliance
Lightning Source LLC
LaVergne TN
LVHW050438211224
799577LV00012B/730